D1246598

THE CLUB OF ANGELS

Luis Fernando Verissimo

The club of Angels

Translated from the Portuguese by
MARGARET JULL COSTA

A NEW DIRECTIONS BOOK

Published by arrangement with Dr. Ray-Güde Mertin, Literarische Agentur, Germany, and
the Harvill Press, London.

Internal illustrations by Nelly Dimitranova, courtesy of the author and Eastwing

Manufactured in the United States of America
New Directions Books are printed on acid-free paper.
First published by New Directions in a cloth edition in 2002.
Published simultaneously in Canada by Penguin Books Canada Limited.

Library of Congress Cataloging-in-Publication Data

Verissimo, Luis Fernando, 1936-
        [Clube dos anjos. English]
        The club of angels / Luis Fernando Verissimo ; translated from the Portuguese
        by Margaret Jull Costa.
              p. cm.
        ISBN 0-8112-1500-8
                I. Costa, Margaret Jull.   II. Title

        PQ9698.32.E73 C5813 2002
        869.3'42—dc21   2001054673

New Directions Books are published for James Laughlin
by New Directions Publishing Corporation
80 Eighth Avenue, New York 10011

All desire is a desire for death.

A possible Japanese maxim

THE CLUB OF ANGELS

1 *The Meeting*

LUCÍDIO IS NOT ONE OF THE DEVIL'S 117 NAMES, nor did I conjure him up from the depths so that he could punish us. When I first mentioned him to the group, someone said: "You're making this up!", but it's not true, I'm innocent – well, as innocent as an author can be. Mystery stories always consist of tedious searches for the guilty party, when it's obvious that there is only one guilty party. Don't bother glancing at the last page of the book, dear reader, for the name is on the cover: it's the author. In this instance, you might suspect that I am rather more than the mere intellectual author of the crimes described within, that my fingers not only tapped out their lugubrious dance over the keys, but also added the poison to the food and interfered rather more in the plot than they should have done. Such suspicions are based on logic, or, rather, on the peculiar logic of mystery stories: if only one person is left alive at the end, there is your criminal; if two people are left alive, but one is invented, the other one must be the criminal. Lucídio and I are the only survivors of this story, and if I didn't invent him, and as it's highly unlikely that he invented me, he is obviously the guilty one, given that he was the cook and everyone died, in one way or another, from what they ate. If I invented him, then the guilt falls entirely on me. I cannot even allege that if Lucídio is an invention, then the whole story is an invention, and that there are, therefore, no crimes and no criminals. Fiction is not an extenuating circumstance. Imagination is no excuse. We all have murderous thoughts, but only that monster, the author, sets his crimes down on paper and publishes them. I may not have killed my nine confrères and brothers-in-obsession, but I am guilty of the fiction of having killed them. In order to prove that I am innocent of these terrible crimes, I must convince you that I did not invent Lucídio. I also need to convince you that the story is true in order to prove that I am innocent of having created a fiction. An invented crime is far worse than any real crime. A real crime could, after all, be accidental or the product of a moment of passion, but whoever heard of an unpremeditated fictitious crime?

I can give the time, day, month and place of our first meeting. If you want witnesses, go and ask the people at the wine merchant's. They know me; I spend a small fortune on wine in their shop every month. Ask them about Dr Daniel, the fat fellow who likes St-Estèphe wines. I'm not, in fact, a doctor, but I am rich, which is why they deferentially call me "Doctor". When he approached me in their Bordeaux section, in February, exactly nine months ago, they must have noticed the contrast between Lucídio and me. He's short and thin, with a head much too big for his body, but he's always very elegantly dressed in suit and tie. I'm tall and stout, I wear a baggy shirt outside my trousers and have even been known to wear espadrilles to the Ducasse de Paris. The people in the shop must have noticed the disparity between us and commented on it. And they will tell you that the place was empty and that we started talking by the Bordeaux and walked around the entire shop together, and that, by the time we had reached the Chilean wines, we were like old friends. They might recall that I bought a Cahors, which I would never normally buy, on his recommendation. And that we left the shop together. We were seen. Lucídio exists. I swear it. Ask at the wine merchant's.

The people at the shop don't know that, afterwards, we went and had a coffee in the shopping mall and sat down to continue our conversation, since we had so many interests in common. Not that we actually got beyond food and drink during that first encounter. Lucídio moves very discreetly and makes very few gestures. He sits with his

3

back straight and keeps his head almost perfectly still. I don't so much sit down on a chair or at a table as moor there. A difficult process, given the scarcity of tug boats. On that day, before settling safely on the chair and calling for the waiter, I managed to knock over a sugar bowl, almost overturn the table and drop the wine. Poor Lívia, my girlfriend, says that I'm not aware of how much space I take up, and that this comes from my having been a spoiled, fat child. Something to do with being an only child for whom no one ever set any boundaries. Poor Lívia is a psychologist and a nutritionist and has been trying to save me for years now. I'm not so much a lover as a cause. I've had three wives, all three of whom were after my money. Lívia isn't after my money. She wants to be the woman who rescues me, which strikes me as a much more self-interested and frightening ambition. Perhaps that is why I resist marrying her, whereas I put up no resistance at all to marrying the others, even though I knew perfectly well that they didn't love me for my belly. We live separately, but she takes care of my apartment and my clothes and tries, in vain, to take care of my diet too. I am convinced that, if she could, she would limit my food intake to the milk from her breasts and to fibre, lots of fibre. I also talk too loudly and too much, another consequence of a childhood without boundaries. Lívia has persuaded me that the whole tragedy of my life can be put down to the lack of someone who would tell me: "Daniel, stop it!"

I remember that I did nearly all the talking during that first meeting with Lucídio. I told him about our club. I told him the names of all the members, and Lucídio responded to each name with an "Ah" or an "Hm", to show that he was impressed. After all, I did cite nine of the best-known families in the state. And, finally, I told him my name, which also impressed him. Or rather, he made some other polite noise, always maintaining the same, tight little smile. Oddly enough, Lucídio never shows his teeth.

Wait, now that I think of it, he said "I know!" When I gave him my full name, Daniel, plus my family name, he said "I know!" Which only proves, you must be thinking, that the meeting was not pure chance. But he might have recognized me from a photograph. Years before, when Ramos was in charge of our lives, we were often mentioned in the press – in the society pages or in specialist food and drink magazines. He might have recognized us from photographs, all ten of us, from photographs and by reputation. We still met once a month for supper. For ten months of the year, from March to December. We ate at a different member's home each month, and that member was responsible for providing supper. We would be starting a new season in March, and I was in charge of the first supper of the year. But there was a possibility that the season would not even begin. Lucídio asked why.

"The group is falling apart. We've lost our pizzazz."

"How long have these meetings been going on?"

"Twenty-one years. Twenty-two this year."

"Always with the same members?"

"Yes. No. One died and was replaced. But there are always ten members."

"Are you all more or less the same age?"

From the tone of his questions, Lucídio might have been making notes on the table. At the time, however, I didn't notice that interrogational tone. I told him everything. I told him the history of the Beef Stew Club. Lucídio only interrupted his otherwise constant, tight-lipped smile to say "Ah" or "Hm".

We were all about the same age. We were all pretty rich, although our fortunes had fluctuated over the past twenty years. They were all inherited fortunes, subject to the inconstancies of our characters and of the market. Mine had survived three disastrous marriages and a life devoted to strange stories, which I collect, and to graceless idleness, but only because my father pays me not to drag any of the family businesses into my destructive orbit. Apart from Ramos, we were all about the same age and from the same social class. And apart from Samuel and Ramos, we had all grown up together. Pedro, Paulo, Saulo, Marcos, Tiago, João, Abel, and me. From almost daily get-togethers in Alberi's bar during adolescence, and Alberi's beef stew with egg

6

farofa and fried banana which, for years, defined our culinary tastes, we had progressed to weekly suppers at different restaurants, then to monthly meetings in our respective homes. And with time and Ramos' lectures, we had refined our tastes. However, Samuel still insisted that nothing in life could compare with a fried banana.

"Does the host always do the cooking?"

"Not necessarily. He can if he wants, or he can serve up food made by someone else. But he is responsible for the quality of the meal. And of the wines."

"So what happened? I don't understand."

"What do you mean, what happened?"

"The pizzazz. You said you'd lost your pizzazz."

"Oh, right. I think it happened when Ramos died . . . because Ramos was the one who died. He was our organizer. He drew up the statutes, had the headed notepaper and the cards printed. He even designed the club's coat of arms. He took it all very seriously. After he died . . . "

"Of AIDS."

"That's right. Everything changed. The final supper of the season last year was terrible. It was as if we were all sick to death of each other's faces. It took place at the Chocolate Kid's apartment, at Tiago's. The meal was excellent, but the supper ended badly. A fight even broke out amongst the women. And that was the last supper of the year, which is always a special occasion. Around Christmas time. I think that in the last two years since Ramos died . . ."

"You've been losing motivation."

"Yes, motivation, oomph, pizzazz."

"Everything but your hunger."

"Everything but our hunger."

The late-night shoppers were beginning to arrive. We ordered two more coffees. As usual, I filled mine with sugar, spilling some in the saucer. I realized that I was recounting not only the slow disintegration of our group, but also the biography of our hunger, what had happened to it and to us over a period of twenty-one years.

In the beginning, it wasn't just the pleasure of eating, drinking and being together that united us. There was a degree of ostentation as well. Once we had exchanged Alberi's beef stew for finer things, our suppers turned into rituals of power, even though we didn't know it at the time. We could afford to eat and drink well, and so we ate and drank only the best and made a point of being seen and heard exercising that privilege. But it wasn't only that either. We weren't just stupid s.o.b.'s. We were different and, at those noisy celebrations of our shared tastes, we revelled in our friendship and our singularity. We had a greater appreciation of life and its pleasures, and what truly united us was the certainty that our hunger represented all the appetites which the world would, one day, arouse in us. We were so voracious, at the start, that anything less than the world would have been tantamount to coitus interruptus. We wanted the world, but we ended up as mere city-bound failures, rolling around in our own shit. But I'm getting ahead of myself. Daniel, stop it! We're still in the café in the shopping mall, and I'm sitting opposite Lucídio, pouring my life out onto the table, along with the sugar.

On the night that Ramos decided to formalize the foundation of the Beef Stew Club – named in honour of our past lives as ignorant gourmands – Marcos, Saulo and myself had just set up our public relations agency, once, that is, I had persuaded my father that my days of idleness were over and that I deserved some financial backing, or at least several years' worth of allowances in advance, in order for me to start my own business. We were full of plans. In no time at all, we would be the stars of the PR world. Marcos with his artistic talents, me with my writing skills and Saulo with his gift for getting on with people, for selling things and for creative flimflam. Paulo had been elected city councillor. He had liberal views which sat uneasily with his bank balance and with having us as friends – he used to call us all damn reactionaries – but he was very bright. We were sure that, within the constraints of the time, he would enjoy a brilliant political career, greatly helped by the fact that he had a brother high up in the national security police. Tiago was beginning to make a name for himself as an architect. Pedro had finally taken over the running of the family firm, after spending a year in Europe with Mara (with whom we were all in love), on a honeymoon that lasted many moons, despite his family's repeated calls for him to come home. João, our clever João, who taught us to invest in the stock market and was our supplier of cigars and jokes, began to earn "obscene" amounts of money, to use Samuel's word. Abel, our kind, sensitive Jesuit, who specialized in grilled meat and fish, had recently left his father's legal practice to open his own. Like Pedro, he too had just got married. At the time, his sense of euphoria was a mixture of the guilt he felt at having broken free from his father's domination, his enthusiasm for the new practice, and the sexual shock of marriage to Norinha. Unbeknown to him, she had already slept with two other members of the group, and had even come on to Samuel once. Abel was the one who would occasionally interrupt our self-celebrations by exclaiming: "Magic moment, everyone, magic moment!", thereby, of course, ruining the magic of the moment. Samuel thought that this need for constant epiphanies was a remnant of Abel's religious past.

Samuel. The best and the worst of us. The one who ate the most, but never got fat. The one who loved us most and most insulted us, and whose favourite word was "bastard" which he used to describe everyone, from the waiter ("Oh, Monsieur Bastard!") to the Pope ("His Bastardness"). He was the most lucid and the most obsessive of us all; he was the last to die, this month, right before my eyes, and the one who suffered the most painful death. And finally, there was Ramos, who convinced us that our hunger was not just physical hunger, that we were enlightened beings, that our voracity was the voracity of a generation, or, at the very least, that we weren't just utter bastards. Ramos – "our Holy Bastard" as Samuel called him – always gave the speeches at our meetings. Everything had started with him. He was the one who had brought a certain solemnity to our ordinary suppers and had formed the club out of "the ten people who are sitting around this table, and only these ten", until death or women did us part. Then he dipped chunks of bread in the wine so that we would all chew together and swallow together, as if making a holy vow of loyalty. It was a ceremony whose eucharistic references Abel found most moving.

In the beginning, Ramos was the only true gourmet of the group. He catechized us and imposed order and style on our hunger. He convinced us that the Beef Stew Club's first act should be finally to renounce Alberi's beef stew as a parameter of gastronomic quality. There was some resistance to this. For years afterwards, whenever he wanted to annoy Ramos, Samuel would defend the virtues of the fried banana. But Samuel would eat anything. And, we suspected, anyone. Ramos taught us that we were practising a unique art, and that gastronomy was a cultural pleasure like no other, for no other brought with it the same philosophical challenge by which appreciation demanded the destruction of the thing appreciated and where veneration and consumption were one; no other art could equal eating as an example of the sensory perception of an art, any art, with the one exception, he thought, of actually stroking Michelangelo's David's butt. He had lived for some years in Paris, and the trips to Europe were his idea, with visits to famous restaurants and vineyards, which he himself organized with, according to Samuel, "typical poovy meticulousness". And he was the one who warned us that the moment we allowed women to join the club, everything would go wrong. It had to be those ten people and only those ten, otherwise the charm would be lost and so would we. He really was something of a prophet.

I don't know why I told all this to someone I barely knew. Perhaps because I had never before had such an attentive listener. Lucídio sat utterly still, his hands folded on the table, like a neat parcel which he only unwrapped in order to take another sip of coffee. The tight-lipped smile never left his face. It was getting late. I needed to go home and phone Lívia, who worries about my lone visits to the shopping mall. I lived close enough to walk there and back, and she used to say that, given my lumbering bulk, the only reason

I didn't get mugged in the street was because muggers feared that such an easy target could only be some kind of set-up. I invited Lucídio up to my apartment. I wanted to show him my wines. And I wanted to continue telling him our story. I don't know why. At our Christmas supper, Samuel had quoted a phrase in Latin, from *The Satyricon*. Everything ends in shipwreck. Or something like that. Lucídio had found me in mid-shipwreck, when I was almost under, with only my mouth still above water, full of the desperate garrulousness of the dying. I needed to tell someone about the tragedy of my life and of my friends' lives and I had finally found an attentive listener. Someone who would not recommend that I eat more fibre.

Only much later did it occur to me: How did Lucídio know that Ramos had died of AIDS? Was it simply a hunch? Had he known Ramos and the cause of his death and inadvertently let this information slip? Or was he giving me the first clue as to why he had arrived in our lives in order to poison us?

2 *The Fish Scale*

SOMETIMES I THINK THAT I DID WITH MY
apartment what I would like to do with my brain. I got rid
of all the clutter. The apartment consists of two vast empty
rooms that look as if they were ready for a ball that never
actually begins. On the bare parquet floor, against the white
walls, are two long white sofas forming a right angle, and
at the enormous windows hang beige curtains, my one
and only concession to colour. Or, rather, to Lívia. When
the group suppers are, or were, held in my apartment,
I would place the big table in the middle of the larger of
the two rooms. The table remains dismantled for the rest
of the year, the chairs piled up out on the balcony, and I eat
at the kitchen table. Lucídio, still with that half-smile on
his lips, examined everything and said nothing. The only
possible response to those two great empty rooms.

On the other hand, in my study, with its walls panelled

in wood from top to bottom, I have done my best to imitate the home of a pair of squirrels remembered from an illustration in a children's book and which, all my life, has been my ideal of warm domesticity. It is just as if I too lived inside a tree trunk, surviving on nuts stored up for the winter, and I know that the reason all my marriages went wrong was because none of my three wives understood that their role in my life was that of Mrs Squirrel. Even the lampstands are made of knotty wood, just like those of Mr and Mrs Squirrel. Everything I love is in this room, in a jumble that has resisted Lívia's frequent civilizing incursions. Newspapers and magazines scattered about the floor. My brandy glasses. My bottles of cognac and armagnac. My cigars. In short, my winter store of nuts. Oh, and my computer on which I write the nonsense that so alarms Lívia – like my endless tale of the Lesbian Siamese twins – and on which I am typing these words while I await Mr Spector's second visit. But I'm getting ahead of myself again. My tree trunk is also home to my television, my video recorder, my tapes, my sound system, my CDs, everything I need to withstand the siege of snow and wolves. And a few books. Just a few, on gastronomy and wines, and some unread volumes about advertising that date from the time when, with Marcos and Saulo, I opened the agency and closed it after a mere eight months. Ramos was the only one in the group who read a lot. Tiago would read and re-read the detective novels that filled his house and of which he was a compulsive buyer. Once Paulo had given up Marxism and abandoned politics to work at Pedro's company, he stopped reading altogether. I don't know where Samuel got his culture from, or where he acquired the erudition he deployed in his insults, like the time he compared Abel's suffering after his divorce from Norinha with that of Philoctetes, whose gaping, suppurating wound so disgusted his companions on the Odyssey that they abandoned him on a desert island. "Keep your stench to yourself, Philoctetes," Samuel would say to the snivelling Abel, while we did our best to console him. Yet it was to Samuel, during long nights in bars or walking the streets, that Abel poured out his hurt and anger until he had managed to purge Norinha from his life. "There's nothing quite like the confessional, even for a lapsed Catholic," Samuel said. I never saw Samuel with a book. Just as Ramos never gave us the slightest glimpse of his life as a homosexual, so Samuel concealed his intellectual life from the rest of the gang.

In my study, the only decorations are Marcos' paintings, given to me by Saulo. Marcos' horrible paintings are everywhere. Instead of shelves there are two temperature-controlled wine stores, which I had painted with imitation veins and knots, as would befit a squirrel's wine store. I placed the bottle of Cahors I bought from the wine merchant's in one of these and chose an Ormes de Pez '82 to drink right away, despite Lucídio's protests. Just as I was opening the wine, the phone rang. Lívia. I had forgotten to ring her to report on my day.

"What have you been up to?"

"Nothing."

"This is the third time I've phoned. Where were you?"

"I got chatting to someone at the shopping mall. I've got a friend with me at the moment."

"Not Samuel!"

Lívia had a horror of Samuel. He was the only one who regularly visited the other club members between suppers and tried to keep the group together and our friendship alive, even though his somewhat gloomy figure only served to remind us of what time had done to us all, and even though his sole concern during those visits was to speak ill of everyone else. Samuel still had the appetite of a young man, but with the passing of time he had grown ever thinner. His neglected teeth and the dark circles under his eyes gave him a decadent air which he positively flaunted, as if forcing us to face up to our own reality. Samuel's body was bowed by our failures, his face etched with all our broken promises. Twenty years before, none of us had had the success with women enjoyed by the misogynistic Samuel, with his deep-set eyes and gruff voice. Not even Paulo, who, according to Samuel, referred to his own prick as the Vote Catcher and used it to recruit female voters of every age and type, anywhere and at any

17

time, the bastard. Once, we had had to bring our collective influence to bear in order to get Samuel out of jail because a woman he had beaten up turned out to have friends in high places and had complained to the police. Pedro had argued that we should just leave him there, to teach him a lesson. Perhaps he knew that Samuel had done what everyone else in the group, with the exception of Ramos, had wanted to do: to screw Pedro's wife, Mara, she of the white skin and the long, straight hair. We vetoed the idea of any kind of exemplary punishment for Samuel. The Beef Stew Club looked after its own. It wasn't just a question of getting Samuel off the hook. It was a matter of testing our influence in the city. Samuel had already told me that he was impotent and that even beating up a woman no longer excited him. He even brandished his impotence as a condemnation of all the experiences we had missed out on in the past twenty years. "I did it for you, you bastards. My flaccid cock is the Christ of this group, dead on the cross. It became impotent for your sakes!" Lívia was convinced that Samuel was a malignant worm who wanted to grab me by the ankle and drag me into his subterranean labyrinth, close to hell and far from her. "He even looks like a worm," she used to say.

"No, Lívia, it's not Samuel."

"So who is it, Zi?"

Zi is short for Zinho which is short for Danielzinho. I have found my Mrs Squirrel.

18

"No one you've met."

I almost told her that the person with me was, in fact, an anti-Samuel. A new friend who was polite, kind and elegant, who was also, I presumed, possessed of a good set of teeth, and was no threat to anyone.

Little did I know.

That was the night, towards the end of February last year, when Lucídio showed me the fish scale. A small laminated fish scale, about two centimetres long, with an ideogram painted in white on the plastic, in contrast to the red of the fish scale itself. He removed it carefully from his wallet. I don't know if he always carried the fish scale about in his wallet or if he had rehearsed that moment. Lucídio held the fish scale before my eyes and said:

"I am the only man in the Western World who has one of these."

"What is it?"

"It's a scale from a fugu fish. I belong to a secret society that meets once a year in Kushimoto in Japan to eat fresh fugu. I and a Chinese man are the only non-Japanese members of the society. Or, rather, we were. He died at the last meeting."

"How?"

"He was poisoned. The fugu is a poisonous fish. If it's not prepared by an expert, trained to cut up the fish in a certain way, it can kill within minutes. The Chinese man took eight minutes to die. It was a horrible death."

I smiled. At least, I think I did. Just to see if this was all a joke. But Lucídio's half-smile had vanished. It was no joke. He went on:

"It takes three years to train a fugu chef. Every year, the society sets a kind of final examination to find out who will receive the title of fugu master. It's always a class of ten students. Each student uses a volunteer to taste the fresh fugu he has prepared for the examination. If the fish has been badly prepared, the volunteer dies in a matter of minutes."

"And what happens to the student?"

"He repeats the year."

"And the society is made up of these volunteers . . . "

"Exactly. A society of ten members. Since the failure rate on the course is thirty per cent, and an average of three volunteers dies at each examination, the membership is constantly being renewed. But there's a waiting list of people wanting to join the society. I had to wait seven years."

"Does the volunteer gain anything from taking part in the test?"

He smiled. This time it was almost a proper smile.

"I wouldn't have expected such a question from you . . . "

"So why . . . "

"There is nothing in the world that can compare with the taste of raw fugu, Daniel. And the pleasure of eating fugu is tripled by the risk you run of dying. The prospect of dying at any moment, in seconds, produces a chemical reaction that heightens the flavour of the fugu. In Japan, anyone can eat fugu prepared by specialist chefs and with minimal risk. But only in Kushimoto, once a year, can you eat fugu with a real possibility of not surviving the first mouthful. There is no comparable gastronomic experience. That is why it is a secret society. It is the most exclusive gourmet club in the world. Officially, the examination doesn't even exist."

"How did you find out about it?"

"I happened to say to a Japanese friend that I had tried everything there was to try and that I thought it highly unlikely that I would ever have a new gastronomic experience. And he said: 'Do you want to bet?' Oddly enough, we too met by chance in a wine merchant's."

"And he was a member of the society."

"Yes. By a stroke of irony, I took his place. He died happy. He had two fish scales."

"Two?"

"Anyone who survives ten meetings, that is, ten years, is given a fish scale like this. He had survived twenty years of fugu tempered with fear."

"What's that written on the plastic?"

"It's a Japanese ideogram which can be translated in various ways. It could be: 'All desire is a desire for death' or 'Hunger is a deaf coachman' or 'The sage and the wise man eat with the same teeth'."

"All that in one ideogram?"

"You know what these orientals are like."

"How many of these examinations have you taken part in?"

"Seventeen."

Lucídio leaned forward as if to whisper a secret.

"And it gives me a bigger hard-on every time."

We drank two bottles of Ormes de Pez and several glasses of cognac, but Lucídio did not for an instant relax his rigid pose or lose his solicitous half-smile, he did not even loosen his tie. When I said I was hungry, he offered to make an omelette and he made an omelette the like of which I had not tasted in a long time. Browned to perfection on the outside, moist inside, sliding on to the plate with the consistency of the nectar of the gods. He had learned how to cook omelettes in Paris, where he had lived for some time. We talked for more than an hour about omelettes and their secrets. I asked what his speciality was, apart from omelettes, and he said that he specialized in classic French cuisine and that, amongst other things, he made a very respectable *gigot d'agneau*. I can't remember now whether I mentioned to him then that, coincidentally, this was my favourite dish. Now I know it was no coincidence. I told him I was worried about the Beef Stew Club's first supper of the season the following month, for which I was responsible. It was an important supper. This was the year that the Club would either emerge from its post-Ramos depression or go under. Following the disastrous Christmas supper at Tiago's house, it might even be difficult to get all ten of us round the same table again, let alone the women. In twenty-one years, the ten members had had exactly twenty wives or partners between us, including my three and Gisela, the adolescent girl whom Abel had adopted after his divorce from Norinha, and the two women Pedro had been with since Mara, including the one who burst into hysterical tears when she was introduced to Samuel, whom she had obviously met before. At that moment, as far as I knew, six of the members had partners. Lívia refused to have anything to do with the suppers and had often asked me to leave the group and use that rupture as a starting point for going on a proper diet and attempting to rebuild my life. If I wanted to, I could go back to work or publish my strange stories.

Lucídio offered to help me with the supper. I accepted, largely because I wanted to introduce him to the others. He said that he would prefer to remain anonymous. He would not be a member of the Club. He would stay in the kitchen. I suggested that he make the *gigot d'agneau*, but he said something which, at the time, I found intriguing.

"No, I'll leave that to the end."

And he went round the kitchen making an inventory of my pots and pans.

*

23

Five minutes after Lucídio had left my apartment, refusing my offer to call him a taxi ("I live nearby") and shaking my hand, at the same time time performing a brief, formal bow, feet together, despite the degree of intimacy which I felt we had already achieved, Lívia phoned. She always phoned late at night to find out what I had eaten and if the wolves had been kept at bay.

"Who was it you had with you, Zi?"

"I'll tell you later."

"Was it a woman?"

"No, it wasn't. I'll tell you about it later."

Who was it exactly who had been there?

Before leaving, and after noting down my telephone number, Lucídio had asked if he could give me a piece of advice. About the supper.

"Yes, of course, go ahead."

"Don't invite the women."

3 The First Supper

THE FOLLOWING DAY, THERE WAS A PHONE CALL from Lucídio. He started explaining who he was, "I made you an omel..." and I broke in. "Yes, yes, how are you?" He said that he was already gathering the ingredients for the supper, even though it was still two weeks off. He had already decided what he would make. *Boeuf bourguignon.*

"Oh, Abel will enjoy that. It's his favourite."

"Yes, I know."

Did he say: "Yes, I know"? I don't know. He asked if I had in my kitchen a particular utensil he would need, and I said I did. Then he asked what arrangements we made about serving the food, would there be anyone there to help? I said that my stepmother would send over some of her own staff. He said he would rather work alone. He would cook and I would serve. I said: "Fine." I said that

I wanted to pay for the ingredients he was buying. He said: "We'll settle up later." And then:

"Have you spoken to the others yet?"

"Not yet."

"Begin with Abel."

That was all I needed. Another Lívia ordering me around and trying to organize my life. But I confess that I rather liked him meddling. He was an interesting man, despite his formality and that awful fixed smile. I could hardly wait to introduce him to the others and see their reaction to his story about the fugu and the secret society. What other stories would he have up his sleeve? I love weird stories. The more incredible they are, the more likely I am to believe them. And it would be good not to have to face that first supper of the new season alone, and to have a novelty to present to my fellow members. Perhaps this was exactly what we were lacking. Perhaps Lucídio would sort out all our lives. Yes, a man who would risk his life for the taste of a deadly fish was precisely what we needed to restore our sense of unity and to haul us out of that spiral of bitterness and mutual recrimination into which Ramos' death had plunged us. After all, we were gastronomes, not a cursed generation or a religious order riven by doubt. Even if he had invented that story about the fugu, it was an inspiration. And if you could judge someone by an omelette alone, the supper would be excellent.

*

26

I began with Abel, who, as I had expected, showed little enthusiasm for the Club's continued existence.

"I don't know, Daniel, perhaps we should give it a rest for this year."

"Abel . . ."

"That last supper was excruciating."

"The main course will be *boeuf bourguignon*, Abel."

"Oh, really?"

He didn't need much more persuading.

"Will you make that dessert of yours? The banana one?"

"Yes, Abel."

"The usual time, then, nine o'clock?"

"The usual time."

Then I phoned João, who also proved reluctant. He might come or he might not. He was actually thinking of leaving the Club. The Christmas supper had demonstrated to him that it was time to stop. "Otherwise, I'm going to end up punching Paulo." In twenty-one years, the only time João had missed a Club supper was when he had had to go into hiding in order to escape some people whose money he had lost and who wanted to kill him, and who thus, according to Samuel, revealed an appalling ignorance of the capitalist ethos. Samuel suggested to the creditors that rather than killing João, they should simply break several of his bones, apart from those he needed in order to recover their money. And he even drew up a list of the bones João would not require in order to earn enough money to pay them all off. But he was also the one who helped João the most, going so far as to conceal him in his own apartment from the furious creditors. From there he would bring us periodic news of the asylum seeker. "He's in excellent spirits. I can't even persuade him to commit suicide." And he concluded with one of his obscure quotations: "One of man's greatest self-delusions is the existence of remorse."

"Why not give it another go, João," I said. "After all, we have been together twenty-one years."

"I don't know . . ."

From his place of asylum in Samuel's apartment, João eventually reached an agreement with his creditors. But he didn't reform. He had been a liar ever since he was a boy and he relied on his inborn talent to elicit money from people and then come up with an explanation as to why the money had disappeared. That had been only the first of the many difficult times that had destroyed his marriage and his good name, but not his good humour and his capacity for telling jokes. At our Christmas supper, Paulo had yelled out: "Oh, no!" when João had launched into yet another joke, and Paulo had accused him of being the perfect stereotype of the Brazilian elite, someone who strolls through the ruins, even the ruins of his own life, brandishing his own inconsequentiality as a safe-conduct pass, as a prior absolution, and he said that to tell one more of his jokes at that precise moment would be simply monstrous. João clearly wasn't contrite, but he might have the decency to stop telling jokes. To which João responded that at least he wasn't a communist who had ended up licking the boots of Pedro, our industrialist, and defending Pedro's company against strikers as vehemently as he had once attacked capitalism during his time as a deputy. When Abel had attempted to calm them down, he too got a mouthful from Paulo, who said he wasn't prepared to put up with his saintly tones for another minute, especially given that Abel was not only known to be one of the wiliest and most scoundrelly lawyers in the whole of Rio state, but was also a paedophile . . . The argument had ended with Gisela chasing after Paulo in order to rub his nose in her ID card proving that she was eighteen years old. In the end, Samuel quoted a Latin phrase: "*Si recte calculam ponas, ubique naufragium est*", which, seeing everyone's aggressively expectant faces, impatient with his damned erudition, he had translated as: "However accurate your calculations, everything ends in shipwreck. Petronius, *The Satyricon*." After a long silence, Paulo said: "Oh, go fuck yourself, Samuel." And Samuel had raised his glass and said: "And a Happy Christmas to you too, Paulo." The supper had ended with Paulo's new wife and the young Gisela almost coming to blows.

"Nine o'clock, then, João."

"We'll see."

*

By the end of that dreadful Christmas supper, only myself, Paulo, his wife and Tiago, our host, were left, all of us very drunk, conducting a post-mortem of the night's events. Paulo had taken my face in his hands and said:

"What have I done with my life, Daniel? What have I done with my life?"

I could barely keep my eyes open. Paulo's wife was asleep on the sofa. Tiago, the Chocolate Kid – the only member of the group who was nearly as fat as me – was dancing, clasping a bottle of cognac to his chest.

"I'm just a pile of shit," shouted Paulo, still clutching my face in his hands.

"No, *I'm* a pile of shit!" Tiago shouted. "Do you know what I am?"

"No, *I'm* a pile of shit!" insisted Paulo.

"Do you know what I am? A complete failure."

"Look, *I'm* a pile of shit!"

"I'm a failed pile of shit. I'm a bigger pile of shit than you are."

Paulo had let go of my face in order to grab Tiago's head.

"Look, I'm a bigger pile of shit than any of you!"

"Why?"

"Because I was better than all of you. I was the best! It didn't take much for you lot to become piles of shit, but I had a long way to fall. That's why I'm the biggest pile of shit of the whole lot of you."

Tiago then clasped my face in his hands and asked my opinion, having first thrown the cognac bottle to the floor.

"Daniel, who do you think is the biggest pile of shit?"

But I was in no condition to make an objective judgement. We were all piles of shit. Years before, there had been a rumour that Paulo had given the security police the names and addresses of colleagues of his in hiding. We had never attempted to find out the truth. The Beef Stew Club looks after its own.

To my surprise, everyone came to the first supper of the new season. Lucídio had asked me for everyone's address and had sent each member a copy of the menu, which he had tastefully produced on a computer and decorated with an old-fashioned vignette, beneath which was a sentence declaring that the supper would be for men only. We hadn't done anything so fancy since Ramos' death. For two weeks, Lucídio came in and out of my apartment, always very proper and very elegant, preparing everything for the big night, showing a devotion to detail that bordered on the obsessive, except that it was a discreet, methodical obsession. Luckily, none of his visits coincided with one of Lívia's visits of inspection. In fact, when I think about it, Lívia has never once seen Lucídio. On the day of the supper, he arrived at seven in the morning and spent all day in the kitchen, which, in obedience with his instructions, I would enter only once, in order to prepare my banana dessert. That was when I saw that he was wearing a huge, almost ankle-length apron and a proper chef's hat. And a tie, of course.

The first to arrive was André, who had taken Ramos' place in the Club. He owned a pharmaceutical company and was possibly the richest of us all, given João's latest financial setbacks and the near-bankruptcy of Pedro's firm. Despite the two years he had been a member of the Club, he was still not properly integrated into the group and had a certain terror of Paulo's verbosity, of Samuel's aggression and of the group's growing tendency towards chaos. He had been proposed as a member by Saulo, who was the public relations officer for his company, and he had had us over for supper at his mansion twice, serving *paella*, his speciality, on both occasions. He was a shy, refined man, much older than the rest of us. The skin on his wife's face was taut from too much plastic surgery, and, at the Christmas supper, she had reacted indignantly to a remark Samuel made to her husband, until André explained that "bastard" was a term of affection. Samuel was using "bastard" in the good sense of the word. Poor André had joined the group hoping to find the pleasant company of civilized people, *"le crème de le crème"* as his wife had said when she first met us, getting the definite article wrong, and he had found himself instead at an endless private party full of resentful guests, watched anxiously by Saulo, who worried about the repercussions our eccentricities might have on their business relationship. I don't know why André didn't just leave the group. Not even the food made up for his evident discomfort in our midst, for the suppers got progressively worse as our misunderstandings grew. But then, as Saulo put it, one could hardly expect good critical sense from someone whose culinary benchmark was *paella*.

"I liked the printed menu," André said.

Samuel arrived shortly afterwards, brandishing the same menu.

"Whose kitsch idea was this? It's precisely the sort of thing Ramos would have done."

By coincidence, João and Paulo arrived at the same time. They obviously hadn't spoken to each other in the lift. João stayed in the living room, and Paulo went into my study. He didn't want to talk to anyone. Tiago was also in a gloomy mood and slumped down on one of the sofas. Saulo and Marcos turned up together as usual and Saulo warned me that he might have to leave early. Abel's first question was to ask if Paulo had arrived, because he wanted to steer well clear of him. He said he was only there for my sake, because it was my supper, but he was seriously thinking of leaving the group. The last to arrive was Pedro, preceded by the smell of his shaving lotion. He lived with his mother, and we suspected that his mother, Dona Nina, still gave him his daily bath. When Pedro came in, some of the group were in the study, watching television in silence, and the others were sprawled on the white sofas in the living room, sad and still, as if resigned to the fact that no one would ask them to dance. If I had to choose a picture to sum up the melancholy end of the Beef Stew Club, that would be it. Only André and I were talking, he out of nervousness and me out of politeness or compulsion. Once Pedro was there, I called everyone into the living room and went to get the champagne. In the kitchen, Lucídio indicated the large tray of canapés he had prepared and ordered me to come back for it once I had served the champagne. In the living room, we gave our usual, but this time somewhat constrained toasts. First, "To hunger", then "To Ramos". Samuel proposed a third, "To our friendship", which was seconded only by André, until he realized that the remark was intended to be ironic. I went to fetch the tray of canapés and offered them to each guest. Paulo asked who was preparing the meal, since there were some very promising smells issuing from the kitchen. I started to say that it was a surprise, but I stopped because, at that moment, I caught sight of João's face. João had just gulped down one of Lucídio's canapés.

To say that his face lit up would be a literary cliché, but João's face did exactly that. He blushed with pleasure. Today, when I think of that first supper and of its consequences, that is the moment I remember most clearly. I was moved by João's emotion, and it still moves me now. For the first time in many years, I had rediscovered an emotion, that of taking pleasure in the pleasure of a friend, and I thought: we can still outwit time, this group can still be saved, I can still be saved. Not everything, after all, ends in shipwreck. I don't know if João was any more of a son-of-a-bitch than the rest of us. That depends on subjective criteria that change with each generation. At that moment, I thought of the João of twenty-one years before, when he had not yet learned that the effect of jokes was lost if he started laughing before the end, with the rest of us round the table hitting him to try and halt his fit of laughter and the whole restaurant bursting into applause when he finally managed to get out the punchline: "No, my cassock isn't made of bronze!" I looked at Abel. Poor Abel. At that moment, he was in such ecstasy that, like João, he couldn't speak. It was Pedro who said: "This canapé's delicious!" followed by approving "ums" and "ahs" from everyone else. I tried one. It was made from grated onion and cheese, but there must have been more to it than that. Whatever it was, I then understood the reason for João's glowing face and Abel's beatific expression. When Abel finally managed to speak, it was to say: "Magic moment, everyone, magic moment!"

The whole supper was marvellous. The canapés were followed by artichoke hearts *à la vinaigrette*. And when I brought in the *boeuf bourguignon* from the kitchen, provoking a "My God" from Abel when he saw it, I was received by an enthusiastic clamour from around the table. They wanted to know who the mysterious chef was. I told them about Lucídio, or the little I knew. Our meeting at the wine merchant's. His perfect omelette, which had led me to accept his offer to cook for the group. And his story of the fugu and the secret society. Someone said: "The guy doesn't exist, you're making this up!" Paulo said that he had read something about such a society, but only in a novel. "It's not true," said Pedro, his mouth full of meat. "He's kidding you." Tiago said that Lucídio might well be a con artist, he could even be an invention of mine, but he was a great cook. Marcos said: "The man's a genius!" and insisted that I bring him out from the kitchen to prove that he existed and to receive the group's applause. "Calm down," I said, having absolutely no intention of leaving my place without first finishing the best *boeuf bourguignon* I had ever tasted in my life. Abel was chewing with his eyes closed. He said again: "My God!" and when he had finished eating, he declared solemnly, provoking loud laughter: "Now I can die." The loudest laughter came from Paulo. The group was reconciled. Lucídio had dragged us back from the brink.

In the kitchen, Lucídio told me that there was just enough *boeuf bourguignon* left for one person and for one person only. I passed the information on. Did anyone want seconds? Some didn't even reply, they just groaned, to indicate that enough was enough. But Abel said:

"I can't resist. I want more."

And I brought the final helping of *boeuf bourguignon* from the kitchen and set it down in front of him, to applause from the other guests. Abel emptied the plate in seconds.

I hadn't stinted on my Bordeaux for that special supper. When I brought in the dessert, with the announcement that our chef would soon make his appearance, there was an almost palpable halo of pleasure hovering over the group round the table. My banana dessert did not disappoint and was extravagantly praised. "What a meal!" exclaimed Marcos, and João got up from his chair to plant a kiss on the top of my head. "What a shame Ramos isn't here," said Abel, with tears in his eyes, and everyone agreed. I served the coffee as well as the cigars and cognac. This had traditionally been Ramos' moment, the moment when he would always get to his feet in order to make a speech, with a glass of cognac in one hand and a cigar in the other, which he waved about theatrically. After his death, no one had replaced him as orator in that moment of plenitude, which had never again been the same. Once, ten years before, Ramos had got to his feet and stood for a long time, gazing round at us affectionately before speaking. He looked at us one by one, as if bestowing a blessing on us. Then he said: "Hold on to this moment. One day, we

37

will remember it and we will say: 'It was our best moment.' We will compare it with other moments in our lives and we will say that no moment was ever again quite like this one. We will sate our appetites again, of course, because that is the blessed nature of appetite. It isn't every day that we want to see a syrupy Van Gogh or hear a piquant fugue by Bach, or make love to a succulent woman, but every day we want to eat; hunger is the recurring desire, the only recurring desire, for sight, sound, sex and power all come to an end, but hunger goes on, and while one might weary of Ravel for ever, one could only ever weary of ravioli for, at most, a day." He may have said "Pachelbel" and "béchamel" rather than "Ravel" and "ravioli", I'm quoting from memory. Ramos: "But even if we do sate our appetites as we have now, we will never be sated in the same way as we are now, replete with our own virtues and our pleasure in friendship, food, life – and cognac." Then he had raised his glass and made everyone else do the same. "Gentlemen, rejoice! We are at our peak." Everyone drank. Then he said: "Gentlemen, weep. Our decline has just begun." And we all drank again, feeling jollier than ever. On that night, it was five o'clock in the morning by the time we left the table.

Abel got to his feet. For the first time since Ramos' death, someone was about to make a speech while we drank our cognac.

"I just have one thing to say about your supper, Daniel."
We all waited expectantly. Abel emphasized each syllable:
"It was fucking marvellous!"

Everyone applauded. André was moved. We had recovered our fascination in his eyes. Now this was more like the Beef Stew Club he had heard so much about. Cognac glasses were raised to Abel. In a way, he had echoed Ramos' "Discourse on Plenitude". We might not have reconquered our peak, ten years after Ramos' blessing, but we had come close, close to our best moment, close to our lost lives, close to Ramos. That was what, in a nutshell, Abel had said. Poor Abel. The first to die, just as in the Bible.

Months later, after the sixth death, after the July wake, I had reminded Samuel of the phrase Lucídio had come out with when he finally made his triumphal appearance in the dining room that night, to cheers from the group. João had got up from his chair, knelt down in front of Lucídio and asked to kiss his hand. And Lucídio had said:

"'Let me wipe it first; it smells of mortality.'"

"It was a quotation," said Samuel. "From *King Lear*."

Damn Samuel.

4 The Discourse on Sexual Desire

MY STEPMOTHER ALWAYS PROVIDES ME WITH servants whenever I need them. I know that she and Lívia meet periodically to discuss my life. She has a kind of horror of being around me – I think it's my sandals that do it – and prefers to play her part from a distance, detailing staff from her cleaning and maintenance platoon to help me out as necessary. We had agreed that she would send round some people to wash the dishes, clean the kitchen and tidy up the apartment on the morning after the supper. I was dredged up from the depths of sleep by the buzzing of the intercom and brought slowly to the surface like a recalcitrant fish. I was still groggy after opening the door to two startled young women who did their best not to stare at my gaping underpants, when the phone rang. It was Lívia wanting to know how the supper had gone.

"Wonderful. Absolutely marvellous. The best *boeuf bourguignon* I've ever tasted."

I told her how well everything had turned out. The atmosphere. The reconciliations. The hit Lucídio had made with the group. The talking into the small hours. The general air of animation. All this greatly disappointed Lívia, who glumly hung up the phone. Her prayers had not been answered. The Beef Stew Club had acquired a new lease of life and would continue.

I was just getting ready to plunge back into sleep when the phone rang again. It was Tiago. He had just heard the news from Gisela. Abel was dead.

We were all at the wake, apart from André. Gisela was standing weeping in the middle of a bunch of strange women. Presumably her family. We didn't know where Abel had found Gisela. We didn't know anything about her. She had never made much of an impression on us and treated us with a certain disdain, shocking us on one occasion by bringing along to one of our suppers a covered plate containing a steak *a la milanesa* and mashed potatoes, saying that she was fed up with pretentious food. I glanced round for Abel's parents, but I couldn't see them. Abel had argued with his father when he had left the old man's practice, and his mother had never forgiven him for leaving the church. Norinha was there, clinging to the son she had had with Abel. Her son is only slightly younger than Gisela.

Abel's six brothers were seated in various parts of the chapel. Not one of them came over to us. Samuel seemed even more sombre than usual. As always, he had taken care of everything. When Ramos was dying, even we, accustomed to Samuel's contradictions and to his cruelty, had been shocked by his insensitivity. "I'm not visiting a queer," he had said, to explain why he hadn't gone to see Ramos in the hospital, on the last day of his life. Yet he was the one who had arranged Ramos' funeral, and grief had made the dark shadows under his eyes and the lines on his face even more pronounced. When I started testing out theories about the death of the whole group, it even occurred to me that Samuel had been left to last so as to take care of the funerals and to register the loss of each one on his face, as on an ancient papyrus.

"Was it his heart?" I asked.

"I think so," said Samuel. "He must have had a problem already, but never told us. Lolita over there says he started feeling ill around dawn and then was horribly sick. He didn't want her to call a doctor. I bet you he died on top of her, the bastard."

"It couldn't have been the food," said Saulo. "We all ate the same, and I didn't feel a thing. Did any of you?"

No one had felt anything. It was true that no one had eaten as much as Abel, and no one had slept with Gisela afterwards. It must have been his heart. Nevertheless, I went looking for a phone and called André. No, he hadn't felt anything either. He didn't know Abel had died, no one had told him, how unfortunate, he would try to be there for the funeral later that afternoon. I said it wasn't necessary, the group was well represented. He said he would come anyway. Then he asked:

"Will next month's supper still go ahead?"

The previous night, we had agreed that André should be the following month's host. He had suggested that Lucídio should again make the supper. Or was that Lucídio's suggestion? Whoever it was who came up with it, the idea was received with enthusiasm by the group, especially by poor Abel.

"Oh yes," I replied.

In twenty-one years, we had never cancelled a supper because of a death. Not even for the death of my mother. Not even for Ramos. At the first supper held after Ramos' death, his place was set at the table, and I recited the "Discourse on Sexual Desire" – or what I remembered of it – which he had delivered at the truffle supper. And ever since then we had drunk the champagne toasts we always drank before each supper, toasting hunger, as always, and Ramos too. Yes, the second supper cooked by Lucídio would go ahead, and a toast to poor Abel would be added to the ritual of the newly resuscitated group.

I rejoined the other members at the wake. I told them that André was fine and then, just for the sake of saying something, asked if anything had happened. I'm no good at keeping quiet. João said that, apart from Abel leaping out of the coffin, dancing a few tango steps around the chapel before lying down again, no, nothing had happened at all. From behind her family guard, Gisela was pointing at us. I heard her say:

"It was at that fat guy's house."

Only Samuel and I stayed until the end of the wake. The others left and returned when it was time for the funeral. About mid-afternoon, Lívia arrived to see if I was all right and if I needed anything. She left again having looked neither at the dead man nor at Samuel. Then, suddenly, my heart gave a flutter. Mara appeared. She kissed me on both cheeks and ignored Samuel. The last time I had seen her was when Ramos had died. She grew lovelier with each funeral. I followed her out of the chapel and she asked me about the man standing next to me, and only then did I realize that she hadn't even recognized Samuel.

"Oh, no one you know," I said.

"Did you see that?" said Samuel afterwards. "She pretended not to have noticed me."

When it was time for the funeral, Abel's father and mother appeared and stood to attention next to the coffin. A priest was about to speak. Gisela was standing with her heels together and her arms out, like a ballerina, supported by the presumed women of her family. Norinha stood behind her son, her hands resting on his shoulders. I guessed that the priest was an old friend of the family. He said that Abel's priestly vocation had been lost to the Church, but that at that very moment, his doubtless contrite spirit was returning to it. Abel's mother nodded in confirmation. Poor Abel.

When she walked past us, her arms about her son, Norinha did not even look at us. Gisela glared at us angrily. The Beef Stew Club has left a long trail of resentful women behind it. We have ruined a number of marriages, but this was the first time we had killed someone's husband at the supper table.

For two weeks, I heard nothing from Lucídio. I had given his number to André, so that they could arrange the next supper. It would be a *paella*, that much had been agreed on the night of the first supper, but it would be a *paella* such as had never been seen in Spain or in the Western World. According to Lucídio, his recipe came from an island in the Indian Ocean that had been colonized by the Spanish, and where *paella* had evolved quite differently and had ended up utterly unlike the original, the difference being based largely on the type of garlic used and a kind of spice, a lemon-flavoured grass found only on the island. Luckily, Lucídio had some of that spice, as well as plenty of the giant garlic he needed and which now only grows in East Africa. When, after two weeks, he phoned me, I asked jokingly if any of the ingredients were poisonous, like the fugu. Lucídio did not reply to my question, but said instead:

"I was so sorry to hear about Abel."

"I was only joking."

"It was his heart, wasn't it? That's what André told me."

"Apparently. But you know what it's like, a young wife and ..."

"I wanted to ask you a favour."

Lucídio has no sense of humour. His smile is permanent, but his lips never part. What favour? He would prefer it if that second supper could take place in my apartment. Things were obviously going to be difficult at André's house. His wife would interfere. She had already made it clear to her husband that she would not hand over her kitchen to Lucídio and she had demanded that she be allowed to supervise his activities, with a right to veto. Lucídio would be unable to work in such conditions, especially since his *paella* – as well as being outside his usual speciality, classic French cuisine – involved unconventional procedures for which my kitchen would be much better equipped. I said that if that was all right with André, it was all right with me. It was agreed that it would still be André's supper, that he would pay for everything and bring the wines, but that it would take place in my empty rooms.

Everyone came. André arrived in the late afternoon, bringing his wines with him. Lucídio allowed him into the kitchen, but only for five minutes, in order to inspect the ingredients. Then we sat in the study while Lucídio was cooking, and André asked me all kinds of questions about Abel. Had I known him long? Since childhood, I said. Almost everyone in the group had known each other since childhood. Marcos and Saulo had been my neighbours, they had lived in the same street as me. They were inseparable. We used to call them the Siamese Twins. Tiago, Pedro, Abel, João and Paulo had also lived in the same part of town. During adolescence, the group had become somewhat dispersed. Abel was deeply involved with the Church. We knew he would have no truck with wild behaviour and we suspected that he was still a virgin. Despite our insistence, he hadn't even wanted to meet Milene, whom all of us had screwed. Paulo became a student leader and distanced himself from the rest of the group, who despised politics. Pedro wasn't around much either. He led a cloistered existence. He didn't go to school, but had private teachers, and was being groomed to take over the management of the family firm. Apart from that, his mother, Dona Nina, was paranoid about contagion. She could not bear the idea of her little Pedro coming into contact with the impurities of the world, amongst which she included us. Especially me. Not for nothing had I borne since childhood the nickname, the Talking Sleazebag. When I saw Mara with Pedro for the first time, I guessed that she had been chosen by Dona Nina to be the wife of her son. No one was whiter or, apparently, cleaner. Samuel had insinuated himself into the group, though no one knew where he had come from. He didn't live in the same part of town, and we never found out anything about his family. He entered our lives as Four Eggs Samuel, for he had been caught in flagrante by Saulo in Alberi's bar, the group's informal headquarters, eating four fried eggs at a time. From then on, our admiration for the scrawny lad with the voracious appetite had never ceased to grow. Samuel never studied, but he knew everything. He never worked, but he was never short of cash. He played dice for money with a group of older boys, in the backroom of Alberi's bar, losing more often than he won. He drank as much as he ate and he was into drugs. Once he had slept with Milene, she wanted nothing more to do with the rest of us and followed him everywhere, despite the beatings our idol gave her. And it was Samuel who introduced us to Ramos, years later, when the group, persuaded by Samuel that it was important, indeed predestined, exchanged the beef stews of Alberi's bar for weekly suppers in good restaurants. That was when Abel, Pedro and Paulo rejoined us, for they had not been part of the smaller group who formed the supper group – Tiago, the Chocolate Kid, the Siamese Twins, myself, João and Samuel. It was as if Samuel, having initiated us, had then handed us over to Ramos, in order for him to complete our sensual education and for us to become a legend. At the time, we still thought we would become a legend, that the city was too small for our appetites. We were bastards, yes, but great bastards, princely bastards. We knew hardly anything about Ramos either. He was older than us, had a private income and, as he put it one day, knew a great deal about Shakespeare and about sauces. His relationship with Samuel was a mystery that we made no attempt to plumb.

Our rite of passage from adolescence to maturity took place round a table in a restaurant, when Ramos explained to us why an overdone steak ceased to be a delicacy and became instead a useful object, like the sole of a shoe. This caused a revolution in the life of Abel, our pious griller of meat. According to Samuel, it was then that Abel began to lose his faith. The revelation that the raw was superior to the overcooked functioned as a kind of catechesis in reverse for Abel. There was an intrinsic incompatibility between rare meat and metaphysics, and Abel opted for the bleeding flesh.

I don't know how interested André was in my affectionate recapitulation of the facts or if he was merely trying to show how sorry he was about Abel's death. Once he had discovered that we were not, after all, "*le crème de le crème*", he had shown no interest in our stories and displayed an almost physical disgust for, in descending order of horror,

Paulo's leftist histrionics, Samuel's slow decomposition and my belly. Now I'm sorry that I didn't let him talk more that night, while we were waiting for the others and while, in the kitchen, Lucídio was preparing the last *paella* of André's life.

A memorable *paella*. Preceded by champagne toasts to Ramos and to Abel and by scallops served with a delicate salmon mousse. We were all in a euphoric mood, despite Abel's death. That first supper cooked by Lucídio had convinced us that the Beef Stew Club could be saved by our appetites, even if we no longer loved each other as we once had and even if we had thrown away our lives. No one mentioned Abel during supper. Abel had once again become one of his family's saints, and it was up to us to preserve what remained alive amongst us, what had been salvaged from the shipwreck: our animal affinity, our group hunger, dating back to the days when we used to grunt like pigs as we munched our way through Alberi's beef stew. All we had in common now was our hunger. I hardly stopped talking, even when my mouth was full. André kept saying how sorry he was that his wife wasn't there; she did, after all, have Spanish blood and was bound to have had something to say about this very unusual *paella*. Then João said that banning women from the suppers had been a great decision. A wise decision. It was the women who had been responsible for our decline. It

50

was the women who had got us turfed out of Paradise; without them, our rituals would regain their adolescent purity, we were once again the contented pigs we had been when we used to eat at Alberi's bar. When Lucídio brought in the second dish of *paella* with large bulbs of garlic arranged around the edge, he was greeted with howls of recognition. He was the person responsible for our resurrection. André tried to protest, without much conviction. His Bitinha should be there, she who loved *paella*, she who had studied *paella*. His protests were buried beneath our ferocious grunting. I remembered the "Discourse on Sexual Desire" that Ramos had made over the cognac, after the memorable truffle supper. We owe both truffles and civilization to female sexual desire, Ramos had said, raising his glass and proposing a toast to the female of the species and their glands. The truffles smelled like the pheromones of male pigs, and the sows in heat and in pursuit of love would search out the truffles and frantically dig them up. "Instead of a husband, they found a kind of vegetable nodule – as many young women do today," Ramos had said. The marvellous truffles we had eaten were the result of the amorous frustration of anonymous sows. According to Ramos, all gastronomic pleasure was a co-opted form of sexual desire. We interrupt the organic process of a plant or animal in order to eat it and we exhaust our own voluptuousness, our own perverted sexual desire, in the pleasure of eating. We were gathered there thanks to the destruction of the forests in the Pliocene period when our ancestors, obliged to live on the open grasslands, formed into groups for protection and began to exchange the natural sexuality of animals for human sexuality with all its concomitant terrors. Human history had begun when, instead of coming into season like other animals, the female hominid became sexually available on a permanent basis, a change that had brought with it the menstrual cycle, lunar time and the long flight from the open vulva that was civilization. All male societies like ours – and here, with the hand holding the cigar, Ramos made a circling gesture that included the table, the leftovers and his nine sated fellow members – were small reconstituted forests, artificial refuges in the midst of the grasslands, Paradise regained by man, before the historic decline and fall of the oestrus. When I recounted Ramos' theory to Lívia, she said that, basically, Ramos thought more highly of sows than he did of women. Her indignation only increased when I told her how much we had paid for the truffles.

Lucídio announced that there was still some *paella* left. Enough for one. Who would like it? André hesitated, then raised his hand.

"Could I take it home for Bitinha?"

"NO!" we all roared in unison. A roar from the forest.

André resigned himself to eating the rest of the *paella*

alone. He left the garlic bulbs to the end, crushing the last two with the back of his fork and squeezing out their creamy flesh, which he ate along with the skins. Sitting beside him and pretending to inspect each forkful with close, scientific interest, Samuel said:

"'The gods are just, and of our pleasant vices . . .'"

Lucídio, standing at the table, completed the quotation, as if they had rehearsed it:

"'Make instruments to plague us.'"

I know now, though I didn't know it then, that this is another quotation from *King Lear*. But Samuel and Lucídio did not even look at each other when they spoke these words. It was as if they had rehearsed it.

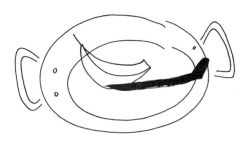

5 The Lesbian Siamese Twins

THERE WAS A SMELL OF GARLIC AT THE WAKE.
I don't know whether it came from the dead man or not.
The eight of us stood in the middle of the chapel, forming a
separate ragged rectangle, like a Roman phalanx ready for
attack from every side. Perhaps the smell was coming from
us. We didn't know anyone there, apart from the widow,
who looked ghastly sitting there beside the coffin, her face
bare of make-up, the absence of which revealed the scars left
behind by various plastic-surgery operations. She did not
look up to receive our condolences. Each of us had to pick up
her right hand from her lap, squeeze it, and then carefully
replace it. André had died in the night. Of a heart attack.

Tiago was at my side. He whispered in my ear, but everyone else in our group heard.

"First Abel, then André ... If we're dying in alphabetical
order then ..."

The next would be Daniel. Everyone looked at me.

"Mere coincidence."

"Possibly, but if I were you, I'd skip the next supper."

"Or take an antidote for poison with you," suggested Samuel.

The following month's supper would be given by Samuel. We had agreed that Lucídio would again be the chef and that the supper would again be held in my apartment, where Lucídio now felt at home in my kitchen.

"What do you mean? No one's been poisoned in my apartment."

"Well, I don't know about that."

"Abel died screwing Gisela. André died of a heart attack."

"Both of them died after a Club supper," said Saulo.

"At which the main course was their favourite dish," added João in my other ear.

"That's just a coincidence. If there was something in the food, why wasn't anyone else affected?"

"I don't know."

The funeral was well attended. There were three grave-side speeches. André had, after all, been a leading light of the pharmaceutical industry. The governor sent a representative; Saulo sidled up to him during one of the speeches and introduced himself. He offered his card. With André gone, he might lose his position as public relations officer for the company and he needed to secure his future.

I noticed that the governor's representative accepted the card, but quickly moved away, making no attempt to disguise his embarrassment at this approach. We were the object of everyone's reproving or merely curious glances. We were an incomprehensible part of André's life. Years before, when the Beef Stew Club's meetings used to make the society pages, many of the people there would have dreamed of one day belonging to our group. Now, however, we were a curiosity, a nuisance. I realized then how odd we had all become. Not just me in my baggy shirt and my sandals, or the gloomy, cadaverous Samuel. Or Tiago, who could never manage to squeeze his chocoholic's body into conventional clothes. Pedro, though a business-man like most of the other men there, looked equally out of place; his immaculately groomed and perfumed appearance seemed almost aggressive, an exaggerated parody of elegance. Saulo had always been a follower of fashion, but somewhere along the line he had lost all sense of proportion, and everything about him jarred with the surrounding sobriety. We looked like a group of invaders from another species who had not yet realized that their disguise wasn't working, and that their tails were showing. I imagine that this was more or less what André's wife used to say to him, once she had discovered that we were not the sophisticates she had taken us for. They're not our kind of people, André. Leave that club of madmen. Yes, in the last twenty-one years, we had all become very peculiar.

Saulo and Marcos were cousins. They had been brought up together, but they couldn't have been more different. Marcos was the sensitive, introverted artist. Saulo was the exact opposite, he had had the soul of a PR man ever since he was a child. When we set up our agency, DSM, the idea was that Marcos would take care of the artwork, I would write the texts and Saulo would get the contacts, but none of us had the one indispensable talent that would ensure that the business was a success – none of us was an administrator. Despite their differences, though, Saulo and Marcos were inseparable. Our nickname for them was the Siamese Twins, later abbreviated to Twin 1 and Twin 2. They used to be my best friends. The increasing bitterness of the last years had corroded our former friendship, and even though Saulo has shown me over and over that he was not to be trusted, I miss them nonetheless. Of all the people who have died, they are the ones I miss the most. Damn, I've just spilled a glass of Cahors over the keyboard. I'm writing this in the middle of the night. Whatever comes into my head. That is why I was left until last, so that I could write it all down. Now I know why I escaped. I am the sacred recorder of this strange story.

Drawing my inspiration from Saulo and Marcos, I began inventing stories about Siamese twins, brothers with completely different ambitions, one wanting to succeed in life as a high jumper or as a dancer, while the other wanted to pursue his monastic vocation; the stories then evolved into the adventures of two lesbian Siamese-twin sisters, stories on which Marcos, Saulo and I worked during the long, idle afternoons at the agency. We had counted on the support of relatives and family friends to help get the agency off the ground. What we didn't know is that everyone considered us a bunch of irresponsible good-for-nothings, with absolutely no experience of the advertising world, and the only support they were willing to give us were a few encouraging words spoken out of consideration for our parents. While we waited for clients to appear, Marcos spent his time painting a mural on his office wall, Saulo in his room, with the door closed, interviewing candidates for the post of receptionist, while I sat in my office writing strange stories or talking on the phone. I talked more than I wrote. I can never keep quiet for long. Then, at the end of the afternoon, the other members of the group would arrive. We had spent a large part of our initial capital on a stock of whisky to offer our clients, but the stock ran out after only a month of after-hours meetings with Club members in Saulo's room, where a candidate or two for the receptionist's job would often agree to stay on in order to meet what Saulo called the agency's shareholders, "the men with the money". Samuel always had the most success with the girls. Anyone who judged the agency by the number of times the lights stayed on late into the night would have assumed that we were working furiously and that our success was guaranteed. But in its eight brief months of life, the agency only carried out one commission, a campaign for a company owned by Pedro's father; the three of us thought it was brilliant, but the old man paid for it and never used it. Still, it allowed us to pay off our back rent and my enormous phone bill. We closed the agency, feeling misunderstood and misjudged, on the day that Saulo's minibar went phut. Without ice, we concluded, we simply couldn't go on.

For Lívia, the stories of the lesbian Siamese twins are a symbol of my squandered life and talent. Saulo and Marcos and, unintentionally, other members of the group contributed incidents and details to the saga of the Siamese twins, but most of the stories are mine. The unfortunate sisters Zenaide and Zulmira, unable to consummate the intense sexual attraction they felt for each other, tried to make up for their frustration by having affairs with other women, difficult, dramatic affairs that were always ultimately destroyed by jealousy. Since they could never be alone with their lovers, one always had to submit to the criticisms and complaints of the other, putting up with the other's muffled laughter whenever she made some slightly extravagant declaration of love or with having her lovemaking interrupted by impatient questions like: "Have you two finished yet?" But the lesbian Siamese twins did not only have sexual adventures. Sometimes one of the group would ring me up with an idea – "Zenaide and Zulmira versus 007" or "Zenaide and Zulmira chosen for the national football team" – which I would then develop. Once I had an argument with Paulo, who accused Zenaide, Zulmira and myself of political and social apathy when the country was living through one of the blackest periods in its history, under a dictatorial regime, with a censored press, with people being imprisoned and tortured, and all those other things which, in our group, only Paulo cared about. As a riposte, I came up with "Zenaide and Zulmira, disillusioned with the political process, go off to join the guerrilla movement", which was a great success with the group of six at the agency, and whose tragic ending was supplied by Paulo himself: in her excitement at government plans to build the Transamazonian highway, Zenaide gives up the armed struggle and surrenders to government forces, neglecting to mention that Zulmira does not agree with her and beneath her skirt is concealing a bomb which explodes as the two of them are being welcomed by the authorities in Brasília. The explosion kills the President and all the military ministers, thus changing the direction of Brazilian history and, more importantly, separating the twin sisters, who can, at last, love each other as they always wanted to, in the midst of the ruins of the Planalto Palace.

*

I continued to make up stories about the lesbian Siamese twins; even today, I'm holed up in my tree trunk writing about them, but the stories are growing increasingly sombre in tone. In my stories, the twins are still Siamese twins, but with time and the twins' increasing age, their condition has become an allegory which I myself can barely comprehend. An allegory of a terrible duality, of our horror of that unavoidable other which is our body and of that excess of flesh which is not us, but with which we share our biography and which takes us with it at the end when it dies, of that ... I can hear Lívia saying: "Oh, Daniel, stop it!" She had found the lesbian Siamese twins quite sick enough when they were merely comical, irresponsible figures. She doesn't want me to tell her what they got up to before we met. Lívia says they are a manifestation of the group's pathological misogyny, which is the black hole from which she wants to save me. I have become a very strange person indeed.

The one member of the group who never understood the lesbian Siamese twins was João. He just couldn't see anything funny about them. He liked proper jokes, not what he called "oh-ha-ha" humour, that made people smile and say "oh-ha-ha" just to show they had understood, instead of giving a good belly laugh. João, our brilliant con man, who had survived for years in the murky, semi-legal world of financial advice and had never once lost his good humour, despite being condemned to death by more than one ruined client. I was thinking about his laughter and his invariable optimism in any situation when I asked Lucídio what the menu would be for Samuel's supper. Would it perhaps be *gigot d'agneau*, my favourite dish? This was another way of asking if the person chosen to die was me, assuming the order of death was alphabetical. No, replied Lucídio. Sautéed mushrooms Provençal – if, that is, we hadn't had enough of garlic after poor André's *paella* – followed by duck *à l'orange*.

Duck *à l'orange* was João's favourite dish.

I phoned Saulo.

"It's duck *à l'orange*."

"What is?"

"That's what Lucídio's going to cook for the next supper."

"So?"

"It's João's favourite."

A silence. Then:

"Phone him."

I phoned João.

"About the supper Lucídio is cooking for Samuel."

"Yes?"

"It's duck *à l'orange*."

A silence. Then:

"Thank you."

João was the first to arrive for Samuel's supper. He saw the look of surprise on my face and said:

"Duck *à l'orange* cooked by Lucídio – you don't think I'd miss that, do you?"

Marcos and Saulo arrived soon afterwards and they too were surprised to see João. Saulo looked at me. I threw up my hands, denying all responsibility.

"I warned him."

"Do you want to die, João?" asked Saulo.

"You're forgetting," said João, "that there are two hypotheses. One: the deaths are in alphabetical order, in which case it's Daniel's turn. Two, the person to die . . . "

João had to stop because Lucídio had just come into the room to check something on the table, which was already set. When Lucídio returned to the kitchen, João went on:

"Two: the person to die is the one whose favourite dish is the main course. There's a third hypothesis too, of course: that we're all completely mad, and the deaths have nothing whatever to do with the suppers."

"Well, we'll find out tonight," said Marcos.

Samuel always served champagne at his suppers. Before and during. We started drinking champagne with Lucídio's marvellous canapés. We toasted Ramos and Abel and, after some hesitation, André too. Then João raised his glass in my direction and said:

"May the worst man die."

63

Marcos said: "Shh!" Lucídio might hear us from the kitchen.

Our chef had a problem with my oven. He had calculated he would need three ducks for the group of eight, but he could only get two ducks in the oven at a time. He would cook the third duck while we were demolishing the first two. The duck was perfect. João moaned at every mouthful. He had never tasted an orange sauce like it. And I must confess that the possibility of dying definitely increased my pleasure in the food. What Lucídio had said about the fugu was true, the risk of dying really did have an effect on the taste buds; flavours took on an extraordinary clarity, and one ate in a state of exaltation, of near euphoria. I remembered Ramos' theory, which he expounded at the last supper before his own death, that there is something in our errant cells that envies the condemned man because he knows when he will die. João must have been feeling something similar. He too was blessed with a destiny, he too was enjoying the strange delight of eating a meal on death row. When I went to fetch the third duck, I noticed that Lucídio had placed a few slices with some sauce on a separate plate and put it to one side. João and I had taken it upon ourselves to finish off the third duck; this was an act of deference on the part of the other guests to the person who, regardless of what criterion was being used, was, hypothetically, about to die.

Saulo sighed and said:

"I'm the one who should die . . ."

He had been fired from André's company. He had been unable to find another job. He had no money and, as well as what he owed his ex-wife, he had to support Marcos too. He looked enviously at João and myself.

We continued to eat like two condemned men.

Lucídio came in with what was left of the duck. He approached the table somewhat solemnly, wrapped in that comical, ankle-length apron. We were silent, eight expectant mutes seated before three carcasses. We knew that we had entered the rarefied zone of grave decisions. From then on it would be the Beef Stew Club against Fate, seconds out, and our adolescence was a long way off. Lucídio said:

"There's a little bit left over. Would anyone like it?"

And João and I looked at each other. I said:

"No, I'm full actually. It was delicious but . . ."

João held out his hand for the plate.

"I'll have it."

King Lear quotation of the night. I looked it up afterwards. Having explained that the secret of his duck *à l'orange* was the Calvados he added and that the sauce was the product of an "*entente cordiale*" – said without a scintilla of humour – between the apple and the orange, Lucídio remarked that he hoped we had enjoyed it.

"'I would much rather be attacked for want of wisdom

65

than praised for harmful mildness.'"

I'm not quite sure how Samuel reacted to those words. I have a vague recollection of a smile, a shaking of the head, like someone who cannot quite believe what he is hearing.

In the latest of my stories about the lesbian Siamese twins, Zulmira, by now an old woman who has experienced the love of all kinds of women, has an affair with a vampiress. She is bitten on the neck and she too turns into a vampiress. She becomes obsessed with the idea of biting Zenaide on the neck, and Zenaide is forced to remain constantly vigilant against her sister's canine teeth, and the unfulfilled love between them turns into hatred. The metaphor, if I understand myself rightly, depicts the horror of a destiny lying in wait for us, as opposed to a fate which, while terrible, is also clear and certain. Lívia puts her hands over her ears whenever I try to tell her these stories. She is trying to persuade me to turn my hand to children's literature instead.

6 *The Fish Scale II*

JOÃO WAS THE FIRST OF THE GROUP TO DRIVE A car. He stole his father's car, crammed seven of us inside and took us for a ride that ended with the car landing in someone's back garden, having first cleared a wall higher than the car itself – quite how we never knew. We fled to Alberi's bar, and, shortly afterwards, the owner of the house, one Homero, turned up accompanied by a police officer. We were all out of breath, and João was bleeding from a cut to the head caused by a garden gnome which – again inexplicably – had flown in through the car windscreen. And it was then that Alberi said the words that we would repeat for years afterwards, whenever we recalled the episode: "They're all angels here." We were not just innocent of having invaded Homero's garden, but, given Alberi's tone of voice, we would always be innocent whatever we did. It wasn't an absolution, it was a curse.

It wasn't a transient condition, a lie, it was a category. And no one looked more like an angel than Marcos, Twin 2, with his delicate features and his liquid, basset-hound eyes. He had fallen flat on his face when he got out of the car and was still shaking and covered in mud, but he was the one who confirmed Alberi's words to Homero and the policeman. We had been in the bar for the last two hours, we didn't know anything about a car, we were innocent. Marcos' eyes saved us that night. We all got off apart from João, when the car was identified as belonging to his father. João's punishment kept him off the roads for more than a month. And now Marcos was the one who was shedding most tears at João's wake. The May wake.

"It's a punishment," said Marcos.

He had grown mystical. Only his weight prevented him from levitating; he too had become peculiar over time. Once, he had tried to drag Saulo off to Tibet and had only given up when Saulo, having used every possible argument to dissuade him, had spread wide his arms so that Marcos could have a good look at him; he had even spun round so that Marcos could take in every detail of his immaculate clothes and underclothes and his ostentatious red tie, and said: "Can you honestly imagine me in the Himalayas?" Marcos had given up the Tibet idea. The two were never apart. Marcos was an orphan and had been brought up by his aunt, Saulo's mother. When Marcos married Olguinha, thus disappointing all the other girls who had fallen in love with his romantic profile and his puppy-dog eyes – or, as Samuel put it, the eyes of a "repentant libertine" – João's remark: "I wonder who will sleep in the middle" was not far from the truth. Saulo went with them on their honeymoon, although he swore he had slept in a separate room. Saulo protected Marcos. He insisted that his cousin was a great painter, even when the rest of the group had accepted that Marcos was, in fact, a mediocrity. He would secretly buy Marcos' paintings, so that Marcos would think that his exhibitions were a success. We all had several paintings by Marcos in our homes, given to us by Saulo. When Olguinha left Marcos for a Uruguayan, Saulo swore revenge, but not just against Olguinha and the Uruguayan. He also dreamed up ways of harming Uruguay by organizing boycotts and anti-Uruguay demonstrations. Marcos was the baby of the group. Not even Samuel could insult him with any conviction, limiting himself to such remarks as: "The libertine could yet become a saint, or vice versa." Marcos was the only one of my friends whom Lívia liked. Once, she had even managed to persuade him to follow one of her dietary programmes. Exercise, planned meals and lots and lots of fibre. It didn't last long. What she did not realize was that Marcos' angelic exterior concealed a diabolical appetite. With the passage of time, our romantic artist had grown fat and ugly and more and more ethereal. He only returned to reality for brief visits, and to eat. He created mystical paintings – banal allegories – but, fortunately, he could no longer find anyone prepared to exhibit them. We got them as presents from Saulo.

"It's a punishment," said Marcos at João's funeral, once he had stopped crying.

"What do you mean?" I asked.

"We're being punished."

"But why?"

Those liquid eyes, the eyes of a now ageing puppy-dog.

"Why? Why? How can you still ask why?"

We were whispering in a corner. The only other sounds in the chapel were the sobs coming from João's family. I looked around me, searching for some satisfied face, but none of the investors that João had conned out of their money was there.

"Look, no one's been poisoned in my apartment," I said.

But Marcos went on:

"We're being punished for our sins, for our corrupt souls."

Saulo gripped Marcos' arm:

"Calm down, Marcos."

At the last supper before his death, Ramos had spoken to us of the secret envy we all feel for the condemned man. He had already known then that he was going to die. So had we. The supper had taken place at my apartment, and

Samuel was in charge of the food and drink. We served Ramos' favourite dishes, medallion of lobster with mayonnaise and lamb with mint sauce. According to him, mint sauce was England's sole contribution to Western civilization, apart from Shakespeare and parliamentarianism, though he never quite managed to convince us of this. Ramos was the only member of the group who liked mint sauce. Ramos said that our lives were like badly told murder stories, lacking any of the symmetry or the epiphanies of art. We knew who the murderer was right from the start. He was born with us. We were born bound to our own assassin. Yes, just like – and he blessed me from afar with the hand holding the cigar – Daniel's Siamese twins. We grow up with our murderer; the identity of our murderer was no mystery. We had the same appetites and weaknesses and committed the same sins. But we never knew when he would kill us, we never knew what game he was playing. Knowing the hour and manner of our death was like being presented with a plot, with a denouement, with all the advantages that detective fiction has over life. Knowing our fate was like stealing a glance at the last page of the book. We read our lives differently, as the accomplices of both the author and the murderer. We had symmetry, meaning and logic. Or, rather, irony, which was a literary form of logic. The only intelligent way of reading a detective story was by beginning at the end, said Ramos, smiling sadly at the protests of Tiago, the Chocolate

Kid, amongst whose many obsessions was an addiction to both chocolate and detective fiction. What we envy in the condemned man is the privilege he enjoys of knowing how and when his life will end. We envy him for being a better reader than we are. There are no casual readers on death row, concluded Ramos. All writers, all critics and all gastronomes ought to live in a permanently terminal state. On that night, for the first time since the Beef Stew Club was founded, Ramos did not call for a toast with the cognac. We all knew that this was the last time we would have supper together. We did not know, however, that the end would come so soon. The following day, Ramos was in the hospital, where he died just before midnight.

Samuel got to his feet and made the toast, raising his glass to Ramos.

"To our own Holy Bastard."

The May wake was the most troubled of all. João's family could find no explanation for his death. He had returned home after the supper, half-drunk, and had refused to go to bed. He had refused to sit down. He said that he wanted to be on his feet when "he" arrived. Who was "he"? João was very agitated. Only as day was breaking did he finally agree to lie down on the sofa. He did not wake up again. A heart attack. He who had never had a day's illness in his life, who had never lost his good humour, who had survived crises, threats of legal action and death and the prospect of imminent ruin, all with the blood pressure of a boy. Of a boy, his mother repeated, indignantly. How was it possible?

Lívia came into the chapel, greeted João's mother and wife and walked over to me as if she were about to hit me.

"What is going on, Zi?"

"Calm down. This isn't the place."

"What is going on? What's happening?"

"Look, no one has been poisoned in my apartment."

How was it possible? Three suppers, three deaths, what was going on? I asked Lívia to lower her voice, but João's wife, realizing that she had acquired an ally, came over and planted herself next to Lívia, right under my nose. She demanded an explanation for what had happened. The Beef Stew Club closed ranks behind me. The Beef Stew Club looks after its own. Samuel said that no one needed to explain anything. It was Fate. Saulo also began to defend us, but he had to stop when he saw that Marcos was no longer at his side. Marcos was standing next to the coffin and had started making a speech to the dead man:

"Sinner . . ."

Saulo managed to drag him away before he got any further, but João's mother had already thrown back her head in shock, gasping for air. We thought it best to withdraw *en masse*, the seven survivors, before we were thrown out. As we left, we heard someone mention a post-mortem. Things couldn't go on like this.

Lívia, with the aid of my stepmother's troops, cleaned my whole kitchen from top to bottom. She changed all the pots and pans and disinfected the balcony. And she demanded to know more about "this Lucídio" who was cooking our suppers. Where had he sprung from? The murderous germs might be on his hands.

I tried to change the subject, but Lívia insisted. She wanted to be there when he next cooked supper for the group. Always assuming we were mad enough to continue with the suppers after three deaths.

A fortnight after João's funeral, Lucídio phoned me.

"I'm so sorry about João."

"Hm."

"Was it his heart?"

"Apparently. There was talk of carrying out a post-mortem, but I don't think they did."

"A post-mortem?"

"To find out what killed him. I mean, he might have been poisoned."

"Poison in the food, you mean?"

"That's right."

He said nothing, and suddenly I was seized by panic. I didn't want him to take this the wrong way, hang up the phone and disappear from our lives for ever. Not before he had made my *gigot d'agneau*. I said:

"Are you still there?"

"Yes."

"Shall we discuss the June supper?"

We had agreed that the June supper would be paid for by Paulo, but held in my apartment, as the other suppers had been.

"Of course," he said.

I gave a sigh of relief.

"What are you thinking of cooking?"

"I'll do quiche as the main course."

"Right."

Quiche. Marcos was mad about quiche.

I gave Lívia the wrong date for the supper so that she wouldn't run into Lucídio in the kitchen while he was preparing the meal. Lucídio complained that the pans had been changed. Luckily, Lívia had replaced my quiche dishes with new ones, though he preferred the old ones. On the night of the supper, once everyone had arrived, I gathered them all together in my study and locked the door. If Lucídio came out of the kitchen, where he had spent the whole afternoon preparing the supper, he would not catch us unawares. We talked in low voices so that he wouldn't be able to hear us through the door. We needed to talk.

"Abel, André, João . . . If it's by alphabetical order, then he's missed you out, Daniel. Why would he do that?"

"It isn't by alphabetical order," said Marcos.

"What order is he following, then?"

"It's by order of sin. Abel was the first of the ten because he left the Church. Isn't 'Thou shalt honour the Lord thy God' the first commandment?"

We all exchanged glances. No one knew the order of the ten commandments.

"What was André's sin, then, apart from being a bore, of course?" asked Samuel.

"And João? The commandments don't really cover being a liar, a usurer, a conman and a teller of terrible jokes. Or do they?"

"It's by alphabetical order," said Pedro.

"Or no order at all. He chooses one person to die and makes that person's favourite dish."

We were all looking at Marcos. Given that he fulfilled both criteria, it was his turn.

"If it is by alphabetical order, why did he miss out Daniel?" insisted Marcos.

"Because Daniel owns the apartment and the kitchen and he's the one who introduced him to us. By any criterion, Daniel will be the last to die."

"The one who dies," said Pedro, "is always the one who asks for more."

"Dies how?" I asked.

"What do you mean 'how'? By being poisoned."

"Look, no one's been poisoned in my apartment."

"Oh, Daniel, wake up. He's poisoning us one by one. It must be the poison from that fish."

"What fish?"

"That Japanese fish he told us about."

"You don't actually believe that story, do you?" asked Samuel.

"Why shouldn't we? He told us that he studied cooking in Paris, and the dishes he produces prove that that's true. He said he has access to a deadly poison and the three mysterious deaths after the suppers cooked by him prove that that is true too. And then there's the fish scale."

"The fish scale doesn't prove anything," said Samuel.

"Why not?"

And Samuel took out his wallet and produced a fish scale identical to the one Lucídio had shown us.

"Because I've got one too."

According to Samuel, these laminated fish scales could be bought in any shop selling Japanese artefacts, and the ideogram didn't mean "All desire is the desire for death" or "Hunger is a deaf coachman" or any other such nonsense, it was simply the ideogram for "sea". And the scale came from a fish that might or might not be poisonous, but it was more likely to be from some ornamental fish. Pedro said that this didn't prove anything either, because the fact was that Lucídio was poisoning us, and Marcos was obviously the chosen victim for tonight's supper, and we needed to decide what to do. What do you think, Marcos?

But Marcos had his head up and there was a faint smile on his lips. He hadn't heard a word we had been saying.

"Just smell that," Marcos said.

"What?" asked Saulo.

"The smell of quiche."

Gorgeous canapés. Giant asparagus, bought who knows where, in Hollandaise sauce. And the quiches lorraines . . . Delicate, delicious, divine. Two per person, filling the whole plate. All the plates returned to the kitchen empty. The only discordant note of the evening was struck by Paulo's wines. Paulo worked for Pedro, who was bankrupt. According to Samuel, the rule in such a situation is for the employees' wines to get worse as the owner's wines get better, because the owner, in order to console himself, starts spending more on luxuries than on his failed business and his employees. The wine was Brazilian wine, which provoked Samuel into insulting both Paulo and Pedro. Samuel was just threatening to dissolve the sleeve of Paulo's sweater by soaking it in the wine, when Lucídio appeared from the kitchen with a quiche on a plate and said:

"There's one left. Who would like it?"

There followed a long, deep silence. Marcos and Saulo were looking at each other. Finally, Saulo said:

"You don't want it, do you, Marcos?"

In order to change the subject, Tiago asked what was for dessert, but Lucídio did not reply. Samuel said:

"Leave it, Marcos."

"Yeah," said Pedro, "let's move on to dessert."

Marcos still said nothing. He looked at the quiche, then back at Saulo, then at the quiche. He sighed and said:

"I want it."

Saulo hesitated, then said:

"Then I'll have a piece too."

Lucídio went back into the kitchen and brought out another plate. He divided the quiche into two equal portions and placed the plates on the table in front of Marcos and Saulo. All this happened in absolute silence. Marcos and Saulo ate in silence and we sat in silence until they had both eaten. Lucídio was standing by the table. When they had finished, Samuel, whose lined face seemed to have grown more lined as the night progressed, remarked:

"'The worst is not, so long as we can say "This is the worst.'"

King Lear. Act IV, Scene 1.

And Lucídio smiled his tight-lipped smile.

7 *Wanton Boys*

ONCE, WE SPENT THE ENTIRE AFTERNOON AT THE agency, Marcos, Saulo and myself, discussing the perfect woman. I was courting my first wife at the time, the one who, when we subsequently parted, touchingly insisted on keeping a little statuette that we had bought together, as "a souvenir of our good times"; when she got to the front door, she turned and hurled the statuette at my head. We had all had girlfriends, steady and not so steady, apart from Samuel, who despised "nice" girls and was a regular visitor to the city's bordellos. But none of those girl-friends had possessed even one of the attributes which we agreed made up the perfect woman. That afternoon, we described her hair and her skin and even specified what her teeth should be like, agreeing that having slightly prominent incisors which pushed out the upper lip – just a touch – would only increase her perfection. We chose tone of voice, breasts, legs, even the thickness of her ankles. However, only when we had described the whole woman and were arguing about whether we would share her or fight to the death over her, did we realize that we had described Mara, Pedro's wife. We quickly devised a name for our ideal which was nothing like that of our friend's wife: Verônica Roberta. We would dream of Verônica Roberta whenever we dreamed of Mara, whom we could never have.

In twenty years, Mara had lost none of her tranquil beauty. She had a few grey hairs, which she made no attempt to cover up. Her body had grown thicker and heavier, but her figure was still our passionate ideal. She looked at Saulo's face in the coffin, then stood for a long time looking at Marcos' face, who, in death, seemed to have regained his youth and his angelic looks. Marcos had always been her favourite. "Marcos is the only one of all of you who is worth anything," she had said to me once, after her affair with Samuel and her divorce from Pedro. She came over to me. Samuel was beside me. The wake for Twin 1 and Twin 2 was going very smoothly, in marked contrast to the turbulence of João's wake, and despite the shock caused by the cousins' simultaneous death and the growing perplexity concerning the tragedies besetting the Beef Stew Club, which had lost fifty per cent of its membership in only four months, Mara greeted me. I hesitated, then said:

"You remember Samuel, don't you?"

She drew back.

"Samuel!"

He was smiling, taking care not to open his mouth and reveal his rotten teeth. The dark circles under his eyes looked as if they had been badly shaded in with charcoal.

"How are you, Mara?"

She was lost for words. They looked at each other, Mara open-mouthed, Samuel's forced smile making his hollow cheeks seem even hollower. Then he shrugged, as if exempting himself of all blame for the passage of time and apologising for being the third corpse at the wake. And Mara burst into tears.

We never knew whether Pedro ever suspected that Mara had deceived him with Samuel. For us it was traumatic. It was simply beyond our imaginings that the perfect woman could possibly have an affair with Four Eggs Samuel, however irresistible he might be. It didn't bother us to think of Mara and Pedro in bed together. Ever since we were boys, we had happily granted Pedro the right to all the privileges of his birth without feeling in any way diminished. When he began having all his lessons at home, we regretted the loss of a classmate, but we didn't reject him or envy him. When his mother forbade him to mix with us, we understood her concern: we really were unhygienic and dangerous. When Pedro was given his first car for his eighteenth birthday, we agreed to the conditions he laid down if we were to travel in it: only two at a time so as not to strain the suspension and with clean shoes on, and we all felt genuinely delighted with the new car. And when Pedro introduced us to his girlfriend, Mara, with her long, straight hair, very white skin and slightly imperfect incisors – but only imperfect to the point of perfection – we concluded that this was merely another entirely deserved prize that Fortune had bestowed on our Dauphin. Pedro and Mara's honeymoon in Europe lasted almost a year, and we accompanied them in our imaginations from bed to bed. When they returned, Pedro took up his place in his father's company, later replacing his father as director when his father died. In the next twenty years, he destroyed the company, as we had expected he would, and he lost Mara, for which we never forgave him. When the Beef Stew Club made its first trip to Europe, Pedro and Mara were not yet divorced, but he took another woman with him instead, thus denying us Mara's company. We had to content ourselves with dreams of Verônica Roberta, who never disappointed us. Verônica Roberta, for example, would never have had an affair with Four Eggs Samuel.

It was on that first trip to Paris with the Beef Stew Club that Ramos spoke to me, for the first and only time, of his homosexuality. We were strolling along the banks of the Seine late one afternoon, and he told me about his Parisian experiences. He had visited Paris regularly ever since he was a young man, and, at one point, had lived for four years in an apartment in Montparnasse. He went back to Paris every year, sometimes more than once. He had a friend in Paris. A very close friend. Then he corrected himself, as if he had come to a decision.

"No, he's not a friend, he's my lover."

"Ah," I said, just to say something.

"We met right here. He's Brazilian."

"Ah."

"I haven't been to see him this time. It's all a bit complicated . . ."

I glanced surreptitiously at Ramos' face, trying to find some reason for that sudden need for confidences. It was pure chance that we happened to be walking along together. We had no special affinity, apart from the affinities of the group as a whole. He was our organizer and teacher and we all admired him, but we knew very little about him. Samuel had introduced him to the group, but not even Samuel seemed to know much about his private life. Samuel always referred to him as "queer", because of his eccentricities and affected mannerisms. But years later, when Ramos was in hospital dying of Aids, Samuel seemed the most bitter about that confirmation of Ramos' homosexuality, which put an end to our assumption that they were lovers.

"Ah."

"I have another friend in Brazil."

"Ah."

"Am I boring you?"

"No, no."

"Love affairs are always boring, especially complicated ones."

"No, no."

"The infinite variety of human behaviour is not as fascinating as people say. Rather, it is the cause of all our sorrows."

"Ah."

I did not feel comfortable in the role as Ramos' confidant. Why me? Since I was a compulsive talker, I was hardly the most confidential of confidants.

"If they were both sensible people, it would be different, but they're not. They're foolish and cruel."

"Do they know each other?"

"Oh yes, and they hate each other."

Then he added:

"They're my 'wanton boys' ..."

I thought he said "my wonton boys" and imagined it must have something to do with Chinese food, but Ramos explained that "wanton" was an English word meaning "naughty", "mischievous", "bad". "Wanton boys" was a quotation from Shakespeare.

That night, we dined round a large table in one of the oldest restaurants in Paris, and Ramos' speech over the cognac was conducted in French, to the dismay of the majority of the members. And Samuel almost caused an incident by insisting on calling the waiters "Monsieur Bastard". After that day in Paris, Ramos never again talked to me about his private life, and I never asked him about it.

At the funeral of the Siamese Twins, a man came over to me and introduced himself. I thought he said he was an Inspector and, before he had asked me anything, I said:

"Look, no one has been poisoned in my apartment, Inspector."

But I had misheard. He corrected me.

"No, not Inspector, Spector. My card."

His name was Eugênio Spector, and the only other thing on his card, apart from his phone number, was the word "Events". He would like to talk to me, when it was convenient. He had a proposition to make which I might find interesting. He asked me to phone him. "As soon," he said, making an episcopal gesture that took in everything around us, "as you have recovered from your grief." Mr Spector was here a few days ago and . . . But I'm getting ahead of myself again. Daniel, stop it!

After the funeral, we went back to my apartment, where we gathered in the study. The full complement of the surviving Beef Stew Club membership: all five of us. At the funeral, Lívia kept saying: "This is madness, Zi, madness.

86

You must stop holding these suppers." The matter to be discussed was, should we stop holding the suppers or not? The next host would be Pedro. In alphabetical order – since Saulo had chosen to die out of order – Paulo should be the next to die.

"So, do we cancel the supper?" I asked.

"No," said Paulo without a moment's hesitation.

"I think we should take a vote," said Samuel.

"I'm the main interested party," said Paulo. "The supper will go ahead."

Pedro suggested that he, rather than Lucídio, should choose the menu. Paulo disagreed. Lucídio would decide what to make. I suggested that we supervise the making of the meal, especially the last fateful portion. Paulo vetoed that too. Lucídio must have full freedom in which to do his work.

"Be honest," said Paulo, "the deaths aside, have you ever eaten so well in your entire life as at Lucídio's suppers?"

"No, but . . . "

"And there's another thing. If we start interfering in his work, he'll disappear. He'll go away. He'll leave us."

"We're the ones who are disappearing," said Tiago. "One by one. One a month. The Beef Stew Club will come to an end not for lack of a cook, but for lack of members. We're all dying!"

And then Paulo leaned back on the sofa – beneath one of Marcos' paintings which, according to the artist, depicted the struggle of the One Being to free itself from the duality of body and spirit – and said:

"Well, I don't know about you, but I don't really care."

Lívia phoned me to find out how I was. I said I was fine and was going to try and get some sleep. She asked if there was anyone with me. "No," I lied. Samuel had stayed behind after the others had gone. He was deeply depressed by the deaths of Marcos and Saulo and by his meeting with Mara.

"Stop this madness, Zi!"

"Of course."

"Stop these suppers. Denounce that cook!"

"Of course, of course."

When I hung up, Samuel was studying one of Marcos' paintings – one of many donated to me by Saulo – that adorned the walls of my study.

"Do you think Marcos killed himself as an act of self-criticism?"

"Is that what we're doing, killing ourselves?"

"I'm not, are you?"

I remembered the euphoria I had felt as I ate the duck *à l'orange* when there was a possibility that I might be the one chosen to die. The feeling that Ramos had described, of entering a privileged territory where everything was clear and inevitable and one's senses were heightened to the nth degree. The territory of the condemned man, or of the taster of fugu as described by Lucídio.

"Samuel, tell me something."

"What?"

"How come you've got a fish scale identical to Lucídio's?"

"Ask Lucídio how come he's got a fish scale identical to mine. And he lied about that, by the way."

"Where did you get yours?"

"It was a present."

"Why do you think Lucídio lied about the fish scale?"

"He wanted to arouse your curiosity. That whole story about the fugu fish is an invention. He just wanted to get you interested. He knew about your taste for the bizarre."

"How did he know?"

"Someone must have told him."

"Do you think he did it all just so that I would invite him to cook for us, just so that he could poison us?"

"Well, it worked."

"But why is he poisoning us?"

"You're asking the wrong question."

"What's the right question?"

"Why are we allowing ourselves to be poisoned?"

Paulo was the last to arrive for the supper at which he would be poisoned. Lucídio had confirmed that the dish of the evening would be *blanquette de veau*. Paulo's favourite. The condemned man arrived with a large piece of red cloth draped over his shoulders, like a cape. He had been looking for something from his past life as a political activist to bring to his sacrifice and had found nothing, apart from a few mouldy books. He had improvised a red flag and he wore it over his shoulders throughout the evening, during which he was the only one to speak. He gave an account of his political commitment from his days as a student, passing through his time as a councillor, the period spent in hiding, the demonstrations, the secret missions on behalf of the Party, prison, and his election as deputy. And he spoke too of his betrayal. Yes, it was true. He had betrayed his colleagues, had turned them in. While we were living our mediocre lives entirely lacking in grandeur, never even experiencing the exaltation of some great act of infamy, some terrible guilt, he had been on the barricades and had grovelled in the filth. What we had in common was our hunger and our failure, but he had touched the extremes, he was better than us, better than all of us, including those who had died. And while he was talking, he busily devoured canapés, then an onion tart, then several helpings of veal accompanied by a dry white Bordeaux that Pedro had disinterred from his cellar for his collaborator's last supper. And when Lucídio brought in the terrine containing what was left of the blanquette of veal, he did not need to ask who wanted more. Paulo snatched the hot terrine from his hands, noisily lapped up the white sauce from the terrine itself, then put it down on the table and ate the meat with his hands, grunting, just as if he were eating Alberi's beef stew. While the others were having dessert, Paulo sat hunched in his chair, silent at last, head lolling, eyes fixed on the table cloth. He did not look up, not even when Lucídio, to everyone's surprise, proposed making the final toast, Ramos' toast, over the cognac.

"You can't," protested Samuel. "You're not a member of the Club."

But Pedro, Tiago and myself persuaded him to let Lucídio speak. After all, the Club barely existed any more.

Lucídio raised his glass of cognac. It was the first time he had accepted a cognac. It was the first time he had not remained standing by the table, merely responding to questions about the food he had served. He had frustrated the hopes I had had that he would turn out to be a good storyteller, and that he would have other stories like the one about the fugu club to recount. He behaved like a chef grateful to be treated as an equal by his masters and to be invited to sit at the table, but who nevertheless knew his place and maintained due respect. Now he was going to speak. He raised his glass of cognac and, looking at Samuel, he said:

"'All friends shall taste the wages of their virtue, and all foes the cup of their deservings.'"

Samuel raised his glass to Lucídio and said:

"'What you have charged me with, that have I done, and more, much more; the time will bring it out: 'tis past, and so am I. But what art thou that hast this fortune on me?'"

And Lucídio:

"'I am a man more sinned against than sinning.'"

"I don't understand a word," said Paulo, suddenly reviving. That was the last thing he said.

"'Nothing will come of nothing,'" said Samuel.

And he and Lucídio drank down their cognac in one, at the same time.

We agreed that the next supper would be organized by Tiago, but with the same format – in my apartment, with Lucídio in the kitchen. Tiago began to say: "And who will be pois . . . ", but he stopped himself in time. Lucídio exchanged his apron for an elegant jacket, bade a formal goodbye to everyone except Samuel, and left. Tiago left immediately afterwards. Pedro gave Paulo a lift home. Before leaving, Paulo gave me a long embrace, but Samuel refused to embrace him and said: "Get out of here, you bastard." Samuel lay down on one of the sofas in the living room. He asked if he could sleep there that night. I said he could. His chin was buried in his chest and he was staring fixedly at one of my bare walls. I said:

"Lucídio knew that Ramos died of AIDS. How?"

"Someone told him."

"You and Lucídio have met before."

He did not reply.

"Why didn't you say something the first time you saw him here?"

He took a while before replying. Then he closed his eyes, sighed and said:

"I wanted to see how far he would go."

"Why?"

But Samuel was already waving me away, indicating that he would say nothing more that night.

The Chocolate Kid – Detective

AFTER THE DEATH OF HIS FATHER, PEDRO HAD
asked his mother to go and live with him and his third
wife. Dona Nina had quickly taken over the running of the
house and had ended up getting rid of her daughter-in-law,
though not without first accusing her of various crimes
against hygiene, home and husband. We were convinced
that Dona Nina still gave Pedro his daily bath and told him
what to wear, but, on the day of Paulo's funeral, Dona Nina
had clearly failed in her duty. Pedro turned up at the July
wake tieless and unshaven. I felt we were being deliber-
ately excluded, and that the only reason we had not been
thrown out was because they did not consider us worthy
of the fuss that would involve. Pedro, Tiago and myself
stood in a corner, far from the coffin, and the other people
kept shooting us censorious, uncomprehending glances.
Pedro's ill-kempt appearance did not help, not to mention

the woollen socks I wore with my sandals and the fact that I too had not shaved since receiving the news of Paulo's death that morning. Samuel did not come to the wake. By the time I woke up to open the door to my stepmother's cleaning troops, he had already left. Lívia arrived at my apartment along with the cleaners, saying: "I just don't believe it, Zi, I just don't believe it. You actually held another supper. I just don't believe it. Who's going to die next?" Hadn't I sworn that there would be no more suppers? No, I hadn't, I . . . Then the phone rang with the news of Paulo's death. He had lain down wrapped in the red flag and he had done another curious thing: around his neck were slung the trainers he used to wear to play five-a-side football, even though he hadn't played it since he was a boy, and that is how he had died. When he found out about the trainers, Pedro said: "I wonder what I should do?"

"What do you mean?"

"I'm going to do something similar. I'm going to discuss it with Mara."

"What are you talking about, Pedro?"

"Mara will know what I should do, how I should die."

His eyes were bloodshot, his face puffy and his hair dishevelled. For the first time since I had met him when we were twelve years old, I was seeing Pedro out of control of his own image, Pedro discovering what the world would be like without Dona Nina.

"I'll be next, you know," said Pedro.

And he sounded almost proud.

Mara was not at the July wake, but Mr Spector was. He waved to me from afar and said, by dint of gestures and grimaces, that our business could wait, that now was not the moment, that he would look me up later, later. Gisela was there, and she came over to tell us that after all these suspicious deaths, she had begun investigating Abel's death. She would order the body to be exhumed. And we had better prepare ourselves because she was going to kick up a terrific fuss. I remembered what Ramos once said, over the cognac, about women challenging men. All women come from one of two different lines, the Judaeo-Christian and the Greek. Those from the Judaeo-Christian line were descended from Eve, whom God had made from Adam's rib in order to serve man, tempt him and accompany him in his fall and ruin. Those from the Greek line were descended from Athena, whom Zeus had plucked from his own brain, and those women never missed a chance to remind men that they were sprung from the head of a god and had nothing to do with men's insides or with their damnation. Gisela belonged to the latter group.

Lívia was not at the wake either, but she was waiting for me in my apartment after the funeral. And she had recruited an unexpected figure to try and force me to confront my own madness and bring me to my senses, a figure I rarely saw: my father. He did most of the talking during this meeting intended to save me from myself, against a background of Lívia's litany of "I don't believe it, I don't believe it", varying only in the stress placed on the "don't" and the "believe". My father was doing his best to understand. Did I know what people were saying about us? That we had gone mad and were engaged in some kind of gastronomic Russian roulette, that the undertakers were beating a path to our door every time we got together. This had to stop. We were just lucky that there had been no police investigation up until now, or a trial, or a scandal in the press. This had to stop!

And then I said something that surprised even me. I said:

"To stop now would be unfair on those who have already died."

"What?"

"I don't believe it," said Lívia. "I don't be*lieve* it. I *don't* believe it."

My father lost patience with me. This normally happens after we have been talking to each other for about ten minutes. On that day it took a little longer. He told me to get a grip on myself. Was I still writing? Did I want to publish a book? Lívia said I had talent. He would pay to have the book published. Perhaps I fancied a trip abroad? Anything to make me stop this madness. I made a supreme effort and said nothing. Finally, he lost patience. If I wanted to continue with this insane behaviour, then fine, but I wasn't going to do it with his money. If I wanted to kill myself, then I should go ahead and kill myself, but he wouldn't finance it. And I couldn't count on any further help from my stepmother to clean up the mess after one of our macabre orgies.

My father left. Lívia stayed.

"I don't believe it. I *don't* believe it. I don't bel*ieve* it."

"You don't understand."

"No, I don't, Zi."

"It's a group thing. All this is a, it's a . . . "

What was it? I could not explain something that I myself did not understand. Lívia said:

"Oh, don't talk to me about the group. A pack of useless failures who have never done anything but stuff their faces and ruin other people's lives. Tell me one of them that has ever done anything worthwhile. Poor Marcos tried, but you lot stopped him. Pedro managed to bankrupt the family business, João was a well-heeled conman, Paulo was simply unbearable . . . And Samuel is sick, mad. He ought to be locked up. I'm sure this is all his idea. I'm sure of it. I wonder if this Lucídio even exists. I bet you he's just someone Samuel invented."

"No, Lívia. You don't know what we were like before . . . before this."

"Oh, don't start talking to me about Ramos, please. From what you've told me, he was the sickest of you all."

Lívia had not known us before. She couldn't understand. She had not taken part in the rituals. After Ramos' death, the women had started coming to the suppers, and all they ever heard about was Ramos, about his speeches over the cognac, about the unforgettable tour of Burgundy he had taken us on, about the time when . . . In the end, Pedro's last wife had protested: "You sound like the apostles talking about Christ! Will you stop going on about that Ramos man!"

On that same day, after Lívia had left, having extracted from me a promise that I would stop holding the suppers, would undergo some psychological treatment and eat fibre, lots of fibre, all under her guidance, Tiago arrived at the apartment. Or was that on another day? No, it was the same day. I'm not being very rigorous about writing this; for a few hours now, I've been drinking glass after glass of wine; I can't remember everything, but this, I swear, is how it all happened, more or less anyway. Tiago came to the apartment and told me that, after Pedro's supper, he had followed Lucídio home. Discreetly, of course. We wouldn't want to do anything that might frighten off our brilliant chef or suggest that the deaths might have something to do with him or show any interest in his life beyond what his formality allowed. But did I know where Lucídio lived?

"Where?"

"In Ramos' apartment."

"What do you mean?"

"The same building, the same apartment. I saw his name outside."

Tiago, the inveterate reader of detective novels, had decided to investigate the deaths of our fellow Club members. It didn't surprise me that an obsessive like Tiago should already know so much – did I know, for example, that João had had cancer, and that not even his family knew? Tiago was the most obsessive of us all. He wasn't just addicted to chocolate itself. He knew everything there was to know about chocolate, its history, its composition, the possible chemical explanations for his dependency on it. He belonged to an international society of chocoholics who exchanged information about their common passion. On one of our trips to Europe, he had left the group to meet up with a correspondent of his living in Brussels, and he had returned in a state of wonderment. He had been invited to spend the night at the man's house, and not only was there a kind of chest beside the bed full of chocolate, but the chest itself was made of chocolate, just in case supplies ran short and the person woke up in the middle of the night craving chocolate. The occasion on which Milene, who had provided all the other group members with their first sexual experience, had offered herself to Tiago in exchange for a bar of chocolate had long been part of group folklore, for Tiago had chosen to keep both his virginity and the chocolate. Years later, he had sacrificed a big contract in order to attend a chocolate festival in Switzerland, and his reputation as an architect had never recovered. But then he was obsessive about everything. In his house, he had one room entirely devoted to his detective novels, which filled the bookshelves lining the walls and were piled up on the floor and on tables. Once, Ramos said: "Man is the only animal who always wants more than he needs. Man is man because he wants more." The Chocolate Kid wanted everything and wanted to know everything. Even his curiosity was voracious. He told me that he had looked into the story of the poisonous fish. There was a city called Kushimoto in Japan, and a fish called fugu that could kill if not properly prepared, but there was no secret brotherhood of fugu tasters, unless, of course, it was very, very secret. He had not found the laminated fish scale in any shop selling Japanese artefacts, but he had described it and been told that it might be a scale from a hermaphrodite fish, and that the scale was often carried by homosexuals, a bit like the cocoa bean Tiago had on his key ring to identify him as a chocoholic to other chocoholics. Always assuming, warned Tiago, that the Japanese man in the shop wasn't just making this up.

The Chocolate Kid and I went to the building. It was near enough to my apartment to go there on foot.

It was growing dark. It was cold. Only the curiosity Tiago had aroused in me could have prised me from my squirrel's dray, which, lately, I had only left in order to buy wines in the shopping mall and to go to the monthly wake. There was Lucídio's name as the occupant of number 617, Ramos' old apartment. The porter eyed us mistrustfully, largely because of my sandals and socks, but he yielded to Tiago's amiably insistent questions and began to talk. The young man in 617 had moved into the building recently, about a year ago. It seems he had inherited the apartment from Ramos. Before that, he had apparently lived in Paris. I described Samuel – which was easy enough, I just had to describe a death's head – and I asked the porter if he had seen him coming in and out of the building. He said: "You mean Senhor Samuel? Of course. He often used to come here when Senhor Ramos was alive, but not now." Senhor Lucídio was a very reserved man, always very polite, but very reserved. He didn't go out much and he never had guests. No, he didn't seem to have any family. He was probably at home right now. Would we like him to tell Senhor Lucídio we were there? No, thank you. We asked him not, on any account, to tell Lucídio we had been there and we beat a hasty retreat. The last thing we wanted was for Lucídio to think we were prying into his life.

Days later, I got a phone call from Mara. Be still, my heart. She was worried about Pedro. He had got in touch with her for the first time in many years. He wanted to plan his wake and he thought she would be able to help.

"Plan his wake?"

"He says it's a privilege. Knowing the day and manner of your death and being able to plan your end gives meaning to your life, he says. He wants to prepare everything, and he wants me to help him arrange the wake. He said that only I remember certain things about his life, things that even he has forgotten. He's completely mad. He even wanted to bring over the group of violinists who played at our table in Paris, on our honeymoon, more than twenty years ago, so that they could play at the wake. They were old men then and have probably all died by now. It's absolutely mad. What have you got yourselves into, Daniel?"

"Does Dona Nina know about this?"

"Dona Nina has been completely out of it for years. She spends all day cleaning and disinfecting the bathrooms in Pedro's apartment. And now she's looking for the recorder."

"What recorder?"

"The recorder that Pedro used to play when he was a boy. He can't find it, and now she's hunting high and low for it, without the faintest idea why, but cleaning and disinfecting as she goes."

"What does he want with the recorder?"

"God knows. He wants to die with it. He said that Paulo died with a pair of trainers round his neck. I don't know what he's got in mind. You've got to put a stop to this, Daniel!"

Mara's voice in my ear. I had never heard her voice so close to my ear. The voice of the woman of our dreams; it was marvellous, even when angry, even when repeating what everyone else kept saying to us over and over, that we must put a stop to this madness. But it wasn't madness. I knew now that it wasn't. I couldn't say this to Mara, but I understood Pedro. On death row, everything became definite, everything became ritualized. Not even the violinists from Paris playing at his wake seemed such a bad idea to me. On death row, you have gone beyond a sense of the ridiculous, all you want is meaning.

The Chocolate Kid and Lucídio arranged to meet at my apartment in order to plan the August supper. Tiago arrived first; he had news. Gisela was discussing with her lawyers the possibility of bringing charges against me, personally, as the owner of the killer kitchen, since, although the Beef Stew Club had statutes and a coat of arms, created by Ramos, it was not a legal entity. And Tiago's investigations were beginning to reveal things which we already vaguely knew or suspected, but into which we had preferred not to probe.

"Samuel was brought up by Ramos from when he was a boy. Ramos paid for his education and, up until a certain age, Samuel lived with him. When we met Samuel, in Alberi's bar, he was still living with Ramos."

Four Eggs Samuel, our hero. A rogue and a sage.

Insatiable satyr and scrawny saint. The one who most loved us and most scorned us, the one who had convinced us that we would possess the whole world and who was now punishing us for our failure to conquer it. He had educated us through our appetite and now he was killing us through our appetite, very gently. We had never known anything about him. Perhaps because we preferred him to be a mystery. Whenever anyone asked Samuel about his parents, he would tell them that they had died of the Spanish flu. And if someone commented that this was quite impossible, since the Spanish flu epidemic had reached Brazil at the beginning of the twentieth century, he would respond: "Well, maybe it was Asian flu; I didn't ask it for its passport."

"So he and Lucídio did already know each other?"

"I don't know," said the Kid. "I don't know if your theory is right or not."

My theory was that Samuel was killing us with Lucídio's help. Samuel was methodically practising euthanasia on the members of the Beef Stew Club. Dispatching the angels one by one, liberating them from the bothersome company of their body and from their insignificant biography, definitively separating Zulmira from Zenaide.

"I don't know," said the Kid.

"Not that your investigations will get us anywhere. We're all going to die anyway."

Tiago reacted indignantly.

"Speak for yourself. I've no intention of dying just yet."

I was surprised by his reaction. I assumed that since he had gone along with the ritual this far, it was because he was prepared to go all the way. I had even started pondering my own death scene, once I had eaten my poisoned portion of *gigot d'agneau*. It would definitely include my set of flick football and my St-Estèphe wines. And perhaps a photograph of Mara. Yes, Verônica Roberta would have to be part of the allegorical tableau where they would find me dead. And alongside me a note, a treatise or perhaps a novel about suicide.

Lucídio arrived, his usual formal, elegant self. He said that he was thinking of making a selection of soufflés for Tiago's supper. Three soufflés one after the other, with no entrée, and nothing else. I said that Pedro adored soufflés. Lucídio said nothing. Having sorted out the details of the supper, Tiago took the opportunity to try to draw Lucídio out a little. Just to be friendly, nothing that might alarm him. Those meetings of the fugu brotherhood in Kushimoto, when were they held? At the end of the year, replied Lucídio.

"Does this mean that next year you might not be with us?" joked Tiago.

Lucídio remained utterly serious.

"By next year, I will have nothing more to do here," he said.

He will have killed us all, I thought. And once they had killed us all, what would he and Samuel do? Would they walk into the sunrise holding hands, given that they were both brothers of the order of the scale of the hermaphrodite fish? Or had Samuel merely hired Lucídio to do the job? Or did the job include killing Samuel himself, who, in alphabetical order, would be the next to die after Pedro? It was perfectly possible that the whole tableau had been set up by Samuel for his own suicide. The rest of the group would die first. Before he killed himself, he would kill all those who would remember him. He would kill himself and his own posterity. A total suicide.

Pedro's preparation for being a perfect executive had included classes in art history and music, and before finding perdition with us in Alberi's bar, he had been a gifted player of medieval recorder music. Pedro brought a recorder with him to Tiago's supper. Not the one he had played as a boy, for Dona Nina had failed to find that, but a new one which he had bought two days before and then spent those two days trying to re-learn. Yes, he would give a recorder recital before supper, before the soufflés. Playing the recorder was the last thing he had done well in his life. He had destroyed the companies left to him by his father, he had destroyed his marriage to Mara, but he prided himself on two things: his soufflés and his recorder. He said all this to me when I opened the door to him, and he grabbed me by my shirtfront.

He was wearing a suit, the jacket of which was covered in all kinds of phoney decorations. Electioneering badges and the badges of football teams, medals awarded to his father for services to industry, even bottle tops stuck to his lapel. And he was more perfumed than ever.

"The touch of an angel, you know. The touch of an angel. That's what my recorder teacher used to say: 'You've got the touch of an angel.' And that was the very first time I ever played a recorder. I can still remember it today."

I tried to wrench my shirt from his grasp.

"Come in, Pedro."

But he wouldn't let me go.

"I had to sneak out. They didn't want me to come. Mara may even turn up. To rescue me. Yes, Mara, she's come back, Daniel. My Mara has come back."

"Look, come inside, Pedro."

"Daniel, I want you to speak at my funeral, all right? It has to be you. I've sorted everything out. Mara knows what to do. I want you to be there, Daniel!"

"All right, all right, but let's go in now. Everyone else has arrived."

I could get the whole group in my study now. Samuel, Tiago, Pedro and myself. The Beef Stew Club had become mincemeat. There were more people to toast than people to make the toasts. Fortunately, Pedro forgot about his recorder, and we were spared the recital. He had calmed down a little. But when we went to the supper table, summoned by Lucídio, he made a point of saying a few formal words before the meal. He said that we might not know this, but for a long time he had given money to Paulo and his causes. He had even given money to the armed guerrilla movement. It was a shame Paulo wasn't here to confirm this. Paulo used to call him a bloody reactionary, but that was just a cover. And he had been the one to give Paulo a job when Paulo failed to be re-elected.

"Do you know what?" said Pedro, as if the idea had just occurred to him. "I reckon our companies collapsed because of all that money I gave to left-wing causes."

We all knew that Pedro had been an active supporter of government repression and had only taken Paulo on because Paulo's brother, a member of the secret police, had asked him to. But this, for Pedro, was the moment of truth, so why spoil it with the real truth? The Beef Stew Club looks after its own. On with the soufflés.

Lucídio did not need to ask who wanted the small amount of soufflé – just enough for one – left over in the kitchen. Pedro – who had eaten all the soufflés in turn with growing enthusiasm, exclaiming: "They're even better than mine!" – did not wait for the ritual offer of the final portion. He said: "I want more, I want more!" And: "Man is man because he wants more!" And Lucídio brought in the last serving, which Pedro demolished almost in one forkful.

After the cognac, while Pedro was surveying his happiest memories and concluding that his best moments had been those spent with his dogs, well, first his dogs, and then Mara, Samuel looked fixedly at Lucídio and said:

"The art of our necessities is strange, that can make vile things precious."

Act III, Scene 2.

But if Samuel and Lucídio were accomplices in that ceremonial massacre, how could one explain the look of hatred in Samuel's eye?

9 *The Club of Flies*

"PHILOCTETES," SAID SAMUEL. WE HAD BEEN barred from entering the chapel where Pedro's body was being guarded by Paulo's brother, the ex-secret policeman, now a beaming retiree, who begged us to respect the family's grief. "Oh, no," he said, smiling, "not you." Through the open door of the chapel we could see Dona Nina beside the open coffin, shooing away imaginary flies from her son's body and, now and again, adjusting a lock of hair or straightening the dead man's tie. Samuel, Tiago and myself were like Philoctetes, the wounded warrior whom no one wanted around because his wound stank. We smelt of mortality. We had gone from being peculiar to being grotesque, and we belonged in exile with Philoctetes on his island, far away from normal people. Then Mara entered the chapel, without even a glance at us. None of Pedro's wishes regarding his own wake were being respected, and a graveside address by me had been unanimously and vigorously vetoed by the family, mainly by Dona Nina, who remembered me as an insalubrious little boy whose proximity to the coffin would doubtless constitute a threat to the dead man. Daniel? Certainly not! The night before, Pedro had arrived back late from supper, but had not gone into the house. He had headed for the kennel at the bottom of the garden. He had decided to die with his dogs. He had been found dead, with his arms around a boxer called Champion and being licked by another called Jackson.

Samuel, Tiago and I set off to the cemetery on foot. Samuel was even more hunched and sombre than usual; he seemed to age several years with each wake. The previous night we had concluded that we were in a dilemma: it was early August and all the members of the Beef Stew Club who were still due to host a supper were dead. Tiago had even suggested that we declare the year over and the Beef Stew Club extinct, but Samuel and I did not agree. Pedro had already considered himself a dead man and he had gone without a murmur. No one said as much, but it did not seem right to end it, whatever "it" was, in that way. It wasn't fair to the dead. That was when Lucídio suggested hosting his own supper. He would make crêpes. A supper consisting entirely of crêpes. He would pay, it was a gift, a present. And so we agreed that September's supper, to be held once more in my apartment, would be Lucídio's homage to the Beef Stew Club, to its dead and to its survivors, and it would be a simple supper of crêpes.

"If the deaths are in alphabetical order, then you're next, Samuel," said Tiago in the cemetery.

"I'm not that keen on crêpes," said Samuel.

"Nor am I," I said.

"Nor am I," said Tiago.

None of us would ask for more crêpes. There would be a supper in September, but no one would ask for more, which would mean there would be little likelihood of another wake in September.

On that late afternoon, while Pedro's wake was being held in the chapel, Samuel, Tiago and myself, the orphans, wandered the cemetery paths, dragging behind us a silence that was becoming heavier and heavier. I usually find it impossible not to talk, but even I said nothing, and Tiago was making a real effort not to ask all the questions he was burning to ask Samuel. He drew breath to speak a dozen times, but lacked the courage. In the end, it was Samuel who spoke, stopping by the statue of a sword-wielding angel that adorned one of the mausoleums.

As we walked back, Samuel began, in the tone of someone arguing with himself: "Certain cultures speak of a Sacred Executioner. He is the necessary murderer, who plays his part in a necessary ritual, and who is not always understood. He is almost always banished and is only understood later on, when he has become a myth. Cain, for example, who is a villain in the Bible, becomes, with the passing of time, a perfectly respectable figure – Cain the patriarch, the founder of cities . . ."

I thought he was constructing his own defence and so I took a chance and asked:

"Does this Sacred Executioner choose his role or is he chosen by someone else?"

"No one chooses him. History chooses him. Necessity chooses him."

"But who decides that the ritual is necessary? In our case, for example?"

"What do you mean 'in our case'?"

We had stopped walking.

"I mean in our case, Samuel."

Tiago could contain himself no longer. The Chocolate Kid, the obsessive, needed facts.

"You and Lucídio knew each other already, didn't you, Samuel?"

Samuel said nothing. Then he nodded and added:

"Slightly."

"He's the Sacred Executioner, so what does that make you?"

The question was mine. He shook his head sadly. He began walking again, and we followed. Without turning round, he said:

"You simply don't understand."

We arrived back at the chapel as the cortège was leaving. We walked behind the cortège, keeping our distance as exiles. I saw Gisela, who looked away, and Mr Spector, who again sent me semaphore signals, which I understood to announce an imminent visit. We were standing some distance away as Pedro was placed in the family vault, beside his father, unaccompanied by any speech. Mara had her arm around Dona Nina, who seemed quite calm. Her Pedro was finally free of all contagion. Only when the small crowd began to disperse did Samuel, who was next to me, speak again.

"In our case, I'm the person to be executed."

We had gone to the wake in Tiago's car. I don't have a car. I've never been allowed to drive. Ever since I was a child I have shown a natural talent for accidents. It is my only apparent talent. On the way back from the cemetery, Tiago said:

"I don't know about you, but I think it's time we put an end to this little game."

Samuel and I said nothing. Tiago went on:

"All right, then. We'll have our last supper, eat our crêpes, and then call a halt, right?"

We continued in silence. Samuel was sitting in the passenger seat next to Tiago, and I was in the back.

"I think we should denounce Lucídio before someone else does. Gisela is making moves to do just that. She says she's going to investigate Abel's death, that she's going to bring charges. Any day now, they'll arrest Lucídio and us along with him as, oh, I don't know, as accomplices I suppose. And another thing . . . "

"'Wanton boys'," I said.

Samuel turned his head.

"What?"

"'Wanton boys'. Where does that come from?"

"*King Lear.*"

"You're not even listening to me, damn it!" said Tiago angrily.

Here's the full quotation. I bought a paperback copy of *King Lear* in the shopping mall the following day. My English is even worse than my memory, and it wasn't easy tracking down all the quotations I had heard from the lips of Lucídio and Samuel during the past few months. But "wanton boys" is there. Act IV, Scene 1. "As flies to wanton boys are we to the gods; they kill us for their sport." Ramos had told me about his "wanton boys", one in Brazil, the other in Paris. The one in Brazil was Samuel, a "wanton boy" *par excellence*. The one in Paris was Lucídio. Ramos had perhaps paid for Lucídio's cookery course. He had probably passed on to both of them his taste for "Shakespeare and sauces". He had doubtless made them both learn the whole of *King Lear* by heart. And that, judging by what I had seen, was not exactly a proof of love. In the version I bought in

116

the shopping mall, the footnotes explaining the incomprensible words take up a good part of each page. The explanations are longer than the actual text. During the last few months, Lucídio and Samuel had been duelling with quotations from *King Lear*. Whatever was going on, it was something that concerned Lucídio and Samuel. It wasn't about us, about our punishment or our redemption. "I'm the one to be executed," Samuel had said. We were just the flies. We were dying like flies.

My father carried out his threat to stop my allowance. Nothing is going into my bank account. Lívia won't let me die of hunger, but I need to find a way of earning enough money to buy some nuts. I don't know how to do anything. Once I thought of writing specialized cookery books. A guide to aphrodisiac meals, another to meals that were entirely red or white or brown. A book of exotic meals from around the world, with ingredients like dog, monkey, ants, grasshoppers. A compilation of meals made or consumed in strange situations, like eggs fried on asphalt, three-yard-wide pizzas, jelly being licked from somebody's navel. There wouldn't be a market for my stories of the lesbian Siamese twins, especially now that they have entered their final phase of terminal terror, with Zenaide forced to remain eternally awake in order not to be bitten by her vampire sister, and Zulmira distracted by endless ramblings about the human condition, about appetite, obsession and death. Lívia thinks that, since I've never grown up, I should write for children. And I've been trying to think of ways of adapting the stories of the lesbian Siamese twins to make them suitable for children.

Tiago was in a good mood when he arrived at my apartment for the crêpe supper. He said:

"So we agree, do we, that tonight no one is going to poison anyone? Is that right?"

Lucídio was in the kitchen. Samuel was sunk in one of the leather armchairs in my study. After opening the door to Tiago, I returned to the armchair facing Samuel, from which, for the last fifteen minutes, I had been observing his sinister silence. We paid no attention to Tiago, who cancelled his smile, slumped down in another leather armchair and resigned himself to the prevailing quiet. Samuel hadn't said a word since he arrived. After another five minutes of silence, I spoke.

"So, you're the one about to be executed."

"That's right."

"By Lucídio."

"That's right."

"Why?"

"Revenge."

We sat waiting for Samuel to continue, but he wasn't prepared to make our interrogation easy.

"What has Lucídio got to avenge?" asked Tiago.

"Ramos' death."

Tiago and I glanced at each other. It was my turn:

"What did you have to do with Ramos' death?"

"I was the executioner."

I thought he meant AIDS. Samuel had been Ramos' lover and felt responsible for Ramos' illness. But Tiago thought differently. He had no time for metaphors. He preferred his detective stories to be simple and direct.

"Ramos died of AIDS."

"No, he was poisoned. I poisoned him."

I still thought he was talking in metaphors.

"You mean you poisoned him with the virus."

"No, I poisoned him with the mint sauce."

Lucídio came into the study to say that there were two types of caviar to serve with the first course of crêpes, black and red. Would we like both or did we have some preference? We unanimously voted to have both. Lucídio returned to the kitchen.

The Sacred Executioner, then, was Samuel. He had killed Ramos in order to hasten Ramos' death. He wasn't thinking of Lucídio when he mentioned the Sacred Executioner in the cemetery. He was the necessary murderer. Lucídio was retribution. And we were the flies.

"Now, hang on a moment, hang on . . . "

Tiago was completely lost. He asked for clarification.

"You poisoned Ramos, Lucídio found out . . ."

I broke in:

"How did Lucídio find out?"

"Ramos told him. He wrote to him from the hospital, on his last day."

"Did Ramos know you had poisoned him?"

"He asked me to poison him."

"Now, hang on a moment, hang on . . ."

"You put poison in the mint sauce at Ramos' last supper because you knew that only he would put mint sauce on the lamb. Because you loved him and wanted to ease his suffering. Because he asked you to."

Samuel was sitting with his eyes closed, supporting his head with his fingertips resting on his temples. He opened his eyes and stared at me for a long time before speaking.

"I loved you all, Daniel."

Tiago was growing impatient.

"Now, hang on a moment, let's just go over . . ."

"What exactly did you want from us, Samuel? You must have known, right from the start, that none of us would ever amount to much. From the days at Alberi's bar, you knew that no one there would ever be anyone. You wanted to save us, you experimented with all the vices for us, you fought for us, you almost killed yourself for us, you even screwed Mara for us, and we never knew what it was you wanted from us."

"And now it's too late," said Samuel, smiling and revealing his blackened teeth.

Tiago wanted to get back to the part of the story that interested him. If Lucídio wanted to have revenge on Samuel for killing Ramos, why did he not poison him first? Why kill everyone else and leave Samuel to last? Samuel gestured with both hands in my direction, still smiling, indicating that he was giving me the right to reply for him. The floor was mine.

"Because they are both bad little boys, Tiago. Because Lucídio wanted to prove to Samuel that he could be even crueller than him. Because the best revenge Lucídio could take was to kill not only Samuel, but to kill everyone he loved first. We were just the flies."

"And because he," added Samuel, indicating Lucídio, who had just come into the study to announce that supper was served, "is an utter bastard."

And he added, getting up from the armchair:

"In the worst sense of the word."

We drank iced vodka toasts to hunger, to Ramos, to Abel, João, Marcos, Saulo, Paulo and Pedro. Lucídio remained standing by the table as we ate the first course of crêpes, with red and black caviar. He took no part in the conversation.

"And you just kept quiet," said Tiago. "You let him kill us one by one . . ."

"I wanted to see how far he would go," said Samuel, squeezing lemon juice over the black caviar. "Call it morbid curiosity."

"But, but . . ."

Tiago was so indignant he almost forgot about the caviar. He certainly wasn't going to choke to death on caviar.

"And what are *we* doing here, Tiago?" I asked. "Why are we allowing ourselves to be poisoned? No one wanted to miss a single one of Lucídio's suppers. Apart from those who had already died, of course."

"I came for the food, not for the poison."

"But you came."

Samuel had finished his crêpes and caviar. He always ate more quickly than the rest of us. He said:

"You knew, right from the start, that this was some form of retribution, and that Lucídio was the executioner. It's just that you all thought the ritual had to do with you, that the retribution was aimed at you, that you were the sinners. Everyone died convinced that they deserved to die."

"Apart from André," I said, correcting him.

"Who?"

"André."

We had left André out of the toasts. André, sacrificed by accident. The only innocent party in the whole affair.

"But anyway, it's over now," said Tiago.

"No, it isn't," said Samuel.

"It's over, it's over. Gisela is taking legal action. She's going to bring charges. I'm going to take steps too. This madness is over. Sacred Executioner, retribution . . . my eye! This is murder, my friends, pure and simple."

122

Tiago looked at Lucídio, who was collecting up the empty plates, and felt obliged to add:

"Nothing personal, you understand."

After the first course of crêpes came more crêpes with various toppings, which Lucídio placed around the table. Tiago insisted that Lucídio sit down at the table with us, just to show that there were no hard feelings. After all, setting everything else aside, Lucídio was a great chef who deserved our admiration and respect. And Tiago saw with satisfaction that Lucídio ate the food he himself had prepared.

We picked at the crêpes. None of us was particularly keen on them. Lucídio offered to make a few more, but we all declined. For Tiago, the important thing was not to let Lucídio out of our sight for a second, especially in the kitchen.

"Are you sure you don't want more?" Lucídio asked Tiago.

"No, thank you."

"Dessert?"

Tiago hesitated.

"Is it more crêpes?"

"No, it's chocolate marquise."

Tiago swallowed hard.

"Chocolate marquise?"

"That's right. But there's just one problem . . ."

"What's that?"

"There's only enough for one. I didn't have time and . . ."

The Chocolate Kid gave us a look of terrible sadness. What were we doing to him?

"You have it Kid," I said.

"Yes, you eat it Tiago," said Samuel. "I don't want it."

"But I don't want it either!" screamed Tiago.

"Then I'll eat it," said Lucídio, going back into the kitchen.

"Wait!"

Lucídio turned round. Tiago asked him how he had made the chocolate marquise. Lucídio told him in detail. As Lucídio spoke, Tiago seemed slowly to collapse, like someone imploding in slow motion. When Lucídio had finished his description, Tiago was slumped over the table, his arms hanging by his side, his head resting on the cloth. He remained in that position as he said:

"I'll have it."

Lucídio stood by the table while the Chocolate Kid devoured the marquise with tears pouring down his cheeks.

"'Dost thou know the difference between a bitter fool and a sweet fool?'"

I've found it already. Act I, Scene 4.

Samuel got up from his chair and went over to Lucídio. Samuel:

"We have to arrange the October supper."

Lucídio:

"The fifteenth."

Samuel:

"Here."

Lucídio:

"I'll cook."

Samuel:

"My favourite dish is beef stew with egg *farofa* and fried banana."

Lucídio:

"Your favourite dish is *cassoulet*."

Samuel:

"I've changed."

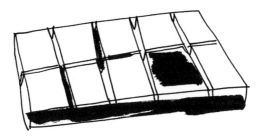

10 *Mr Spector's Visit*

"THINGS THAT LOVE NIGHT LOVE NOT SUCH
nights as these." *King Lear*, you can ask me anything
you like about it now. "In such a night . . ." It was a night
of Shakespearian storms, with artificial lightning and
thunder from a thunder sheet, when Samuel and Lucídio
met for the final scene of their story, in my apartment, in
my empty rooms. At the Chocolate Kid's funeral, which we
witnessed from afar because they would not let us into the
cemetery, Samuel had said:

"Of course I'll go to the supper. I owe it to the group."

"In the name of the group, I release you from that debt."

"It's too late now."

"In such a night . . ." It was pouring with rain, the wind
was shaking the windows, and, when Lucídio came into
the large salon bearing the tray with the beef stew, the
egg *farofa* and fried bananas, the lights all went out. For

a considerable time, only flashes of lightning lit the scene: Samuel and I eating the beef stew, filling our mouths with beef stew, egg *farofa* and fried bananas and grunting like pigs, and Lucídio standing stiffly by the table in his long white apron, with the table cloth and the walls turning blue with every lightning flash, and us washing down the food with Coca-Cola just as we used to do at Alberi's bar. By the time the lights came on again, we had finished. Lucídio asked Samuel if he wanted more. Samuel said no.

"No?"

"Look, don't take this the wrong way, but Alberi's beef stew was much better. Beef stew just isn't your forte."

"Are you sure you don't want any more?"

Samuel took a few moments to respond. Outside in the street, there were cataracts and hurricanoes and winds cracking their cheeks.

"All right," said Samuel. "Bring me another fried banana."

If Samuel had prepared some final words, he did not have time to say them. He died eight minutes after eating the banana, contorted with pain. He was the only one whom I actually saw die. I watched his death agony paralysed, gripping the edge of the table, unable to take my eyes off that body in convulsions on my parquet floor. Seeing Samuel die cured me of any idea of allowing myself to be poisoned too, of carrying the ritual to its logical conclusion. That particular story was over. I don't know why I was

127

saved. Perhaps simply to be the one who survived to tell the tale. The spasms shaking Samuel's body finally ceased. I was just about to stand up when Lucídio stopped me with a gesture. He dragged the corpse over to one of my sofas. Then, as he began clearing the table, he said:

"Call an ambulance."

"An ambulance?"

"They'll assume it was a heart attack."

"But what about his family . . ."

"He hasn't got any family. He hasn't got anyone."

"But they'll be suspicious . . ."

"Why?"

"Yet another death."

"So?"

Lucídio was heading back to the kitchen. I sat down again, stunned. Then I jumped. The ambulance. The phone. Where was the phone? I was in my own apartment, but I didn't know where the phone was. I only found it when it began to ring. I followed the sound. It was Lívia, wanting to know if I had eaten.

"Yes, I've eaten."

"What?"

"What do you mean 'what'?"

"What did you eat, Zi?"

"Beef stew. *Farofa*. Banana."

Lívia was surprised. That wasn't amongst the frozen meals with which she had stocked up my freezer for the week. Beef stew? *Farofa*? Banana?

"I'm coming over, Zi. You sound odd."

"No don't, you can't come out in this storm."

"What storm?"

I looked out of the window. There was no storm.

"I'm fine. I'm going to bed now. We'll talk tomorrow."

"Did you hear about Gisela?"

"No, what happened?"

"She's dead."

"What? But how?"

"Apparently her heart gave out."

"Her heart? At eighteen?"

"That's right."

Lucídio volunteered to tell the ambulance crew what had happened. I was in no state to speak. We had been eating, when Samuel had suddenly stood up, clutching his chest, and the next thing we knew he was under the table. We had tried to revive him, but without success. No, we didn't know his family. He lived alone. Who should be informed of his death? We had no idea. Who would pay for the funeral? Lucídio glanced at me. I nodded. And I began calculating what I could sell in my apartment in order to get hold of some money.

The only people present at the October wake, Samuel's wake, were myself and Mr Spector. Lívia wouldn't come with me. She isn't talking to me, not since she found out about Samuel dying in my apartment. She wasn't convinced when I told her that it really had been a heart attack, that it had nothing to do with the suppers, the group, the madness. Mr Spector approached discreetly and asked: "Cancer?" I replied: "Heart" and he shook his head and said something which, at the time, I didn't understand:

"I'm sure he won't regret it."

I arranged for Mr Spector to visit me two days later, to talk. He realized that this wasn't the moment. After burying Samuel, I caught a taxi and asked to be taken to the district where we used to live. I hadn't been there for years. Where Alberi's bar had been, there was now a video shop. I stood on the pavement staring at the new building and trying to remember how the old one used to look. I caught another taxi and returned to my tree house. If I had been saved in order to remember, then I would do a pretty terrible job. That is why I started to write.

Mr Spector began by saying that he had heard of our "organization" through a friend, and that he was interested in what we were doing because it chimed in with an idea of his own, or rather, it wasn't just his idea, but that of a group of people he represented. A group.

"Interested in what we're doing?"

"That's right. I don't know quite how I'd describe it . . . Mercy killings, perhaps?"

"Mercy killings?"

"Easeful deaths?"

"Easeful deaths?"

"Terminal pleasures?"

"Terminal pleasures?"

"What would you call it, sir?"

"What would I call what?"

"What you do, killing people with an excess of what they most like."

He interpreted my silence as wariness and hastened to reassure me that I could trust him, that any agreement we reached would be strictly confidential.

"Right, hm. Yes. This friend of yours . . . Could you tell me what exactly he told you?"

"He's more than a friend, really, he's my cousin. A doctor. He was treating a patient with terminal cancer who decided, shall we say, to take advantage of the services your organization offers and to allow you to kill him. This friend of mine, this cousin, didn't approve, obviously, although he's not entirely against the concept."

"What concept?"

"Of . . . euthanasia with joy."

"Euthanasia with joy?"

"Orgiastic release."

"Orgiastic release?"

"Going out with a bang."

"Going out with a bang?"

"Sympathetic apotheosis?"

"Sympathetic apoth . . . Listen, what exactly did this patient tell the doctor?"

"That you killed terminal patients in the manner of their choosing. With an excess of good food, with an excess of sex, with an excess of whatever gave them pleasure."

João always was a liar.

"And what exactly are you proposing?"

"I represent a group of people interested in taking part in this initiative."

"You represent a group of people interested in investing in our, erm, organization?"

"No, no. They're interested in using your services, they're interested in dying in your hands."

I must have pulled a face, because Mr Spector added quickly:

"And prepared to pay good money for it. In advance, of course."

"Of course."

I asked for time to think about it. I needed to consult the other members of the, erm, organization. We had never considered expanding our services like that. We normally only helped out friends. We were a sort of club of death in a way. We manufactured angels, but only angels we knew, always assuming that anyone who died in our hands, begging for more, more, more, could properly be called an angel. As I'm sure you will understand, we need to consider the practical details, the moral connotations, the possible legal implications, it's not easy. Mr Spector said that he understood. We agreed that he would come back tomorrow to find out our response. As he was leaving, I asked if Mr Spector was himself ill with a terminal disease and he, with a modest air, said no, he was merely an intermediary. But he confessed that he had often thought of the happiness it must bring to be able to plan one's own end. It would be a little like looking at the last page of a mystery story before you read it. That way you would read it more intelligently.

I phoned Lucídio, fearing that he might have left town. But he was still in the same apartment. He did not have the slightest intention of leaving. Which meant that he was not in the least concerned that I would reveal everything I knew about his terrible revenge. Since he had also eliminated Gisela, though how I don't know, and since I could not possibly denounce him without admitting my own complicity in the affair, all he needed to do was to allow time to pass and for people to forget about the sad demise of the Beef Stew Club. He could then open a restaurant with the money left over from his inheritance from Ramos. I told him about Mr Spector's visit and his proposal, expecting Lucídio to burst out laughing. But Lucídio never laughs. He asked if I was sure that Mr Spector really was who he said he was. He might be a police inspector, perhaps he was carrying out an investigation, perhaps he had invented that whole story about a group who wanted to die of pleasure because he knew of my taste for unlikely stories. He suggested that we invite Mr Spector to supper in order to talk over his proposal, tomorrow. And he said:

"After all, I still haven't made your *gigot d'agneau.*"

Today, when Mr Spector arrives, I'm going to invite him to supper. I hope he likes *gigot d'agneau* too. The more I think about his idea, the more I like it. If Lucídio agrees, we could earn a lot of money, and I need money. St-Estèphe wines are getting dearer and dearer, and I've sold everything in my apartment, apart from Marcos' paintings, which nobody wants to buy. With Mr Spector as our agent, supplying us with clients eager to experience our sympathetic apotheoses, we might even consider expanding the business and making it more like the lie that João invented for his doctor, more like the bizarre tale told by our teller of jokes. I can see us not only killing the terminally ill at grand suppers in my empty rooms, but also organizing Caribbean cruises for the dying, millionaires' tours of Europe's capitals, of Asia's dens of iniquity, of all the world's definitive pleasures, providing mortal adventures, ultimate ecstasies, fatal extremes, supreme orgasms, monumental erections to whoever wants more, always more, and more, more, more, more, more, more, more, more, more, more, more, more . . . Daniel, stop it!